Accidental Pleasure

Sexy Stories Collection

VOLUME 44

14 EROTIC SHORT STORIES

STEFAN MCKINNIS

Publisher's Note: This is a work of fiction. Names, characters, places, and incidents are a product of the author's imagination. Locales and public names are sometimes used for atmospheric purposes. Any resemblance to actual people, living or dead, or to businesses, companies, events, institutions, or locales is completely coincidental.

Accidental Pleasure/ Stefan McKinnis. -- 1st ed.
Xplicit Press, an imprint of TLM Media LLC

ISBN-13: 978-1-62327-575-4
ISBN-10: 1-62327-575-X
eISBN: 978-1-62327-625-6

Printed in the United States of America

CONTENTS

1 THE GOOD ONES ALWAYS COME BACK

Prologue

Summer celebrated her 10-year anniversary of teaching middle school quietly. She lived a simple life, so enjoying a night with friends and a glass of wine and a piece of cake was enough. At 30, she kept her girlish appeal with a slender figure that made her look much younger. That was a blessing and a curse when it came to teaching a room full of ninth grade boys and girls.

Summer had learned a lot about keeping her nose clean. The school district put her to work as a substitute teacher and helper as she worked her way through college. Before that, Summer volunteered at private schools where she developed her lifelong passion for guiding young people in their lessons. Even at just 18 years old, she had learned some of the pitfalls of being a beautiful young woman in an educational setting.

While helping out at the elementary school, Summer became very aware of the dads. Their looks were lustful and obvious. The problem was that every now and then one of those dads was amazingly hot and it was hard not to like how he looked at her. She carefully did not tell her parents this side of her new job, or that would have been the end of it.

Mr. Sandovar

As she went to her car late one afternoon, Summer saw the large luxury car parked in front of the school. She had worked late to help in decorating the gym for a project. Because it was so late, not many people were still around. Summer got in her car and found that it would not start. Frustrated, she got out and opened the hood even though she had no idea what was under there.

Just then, she heard a deep male voice with a slight Hispanic accent.

"Are you OK, Miss?"

She looked up and a gorgeous man was standing next to that fancy luxury car about to get in the back seat. At first, she must have looked a little nervous at talking to a stranger. Then he gave a reassuring smile.

"Do not worry. I am Mr. Sandovar. I think you help out in my little girl's second grade class. Her name is Maria."

Summer relaxed a bit because she knew Maria. She was a gorgeous 7-year-old girl in Mrs. Cox's class.

"Oh yes, Maria is a lovely girl. Is she with

you?" Summer asked.

"No, I just came up to the school to drop off teacher's supplies. I am on the school board. Is everything OK with your car?" he inquired in a friendly way.

"It's dead and I don't know anything about it. My dad has an auto club so I will have to hike home to get the card. But it's OK because it is only a couple of miles."

"Nonsense. Let me drive you home. I have lots of room."

Mr. Sandovar opened the door. Inside the car was like a luxury hotel suite. It was clear that Mr. Sandovar was very wealthy. Summer decided to go along just to enjoy that fancy ride. Inside the car, she was alone with him because there was a barrier between them and the driver.

Summer giggled a little bit at how amazing the limo was. But when she was alone with that sexy and handsome dark-skinned man, she felt her heart skip a beat. His shirt was open a few buttons so she could see his sexy chest with dark tufts of hair. His eyes were dark black with a piercing stare. His skin was a gorgeous brown color that was offset by his black curly hair. Without thinking, Summer smiled at him almost as if she was flirting with him.

Mr. Sandovar looked at the gorgeous, slender blond-haired girl in his limo and his desire was stirred for her. He felt restraint because he was pretty sure he knew her parents and she was just barely over 18. Her eyes were pools of innocence and infatuation as she gazed at him and he was drawn to them. To keep himself from kissing her, he simply put his finger on her lips and caressed it, which only filled the young girl with stronger desire.

"You are quite lovely, Summer. Is there a lucky young man who makes love to you daily?"

Summer was not a virgin. She had lost her virginity to a boyfriend when she was 15. But that first time was crude and clumsy with no romance or excitement. Already her pussy was wet being alone with Mr. Sandovar.

"No. Nobody to love me."

The driver was driving the neighborhood slowly, waiting for instructions but knowing it may take a while before they came. He knew how this worked.

"You deserve love, my angel."

All Summer could do was gasp when he said that and she closed her eyes. She was all his and he knew that. He kissed her softly and that kiss quickly became deep and passionate. Summer felt the sexy man slide his tongue into her mouth, and she opened wide for that. She explored his mouth, giving back to him as she was getting. When he sucked her tongue, she thought she would explode inside.

The experienced lover knew he could not keep the young girl in his car for long. She was gasping with desire as he pulled up her long skirt and pushed his hand under it. Her skin was soft and cool to his touch, and she opened her thighs instinctively as he felt higher and higher toward her panties.

As Mr. Sandovar moved his kisses from Summer's lips to her neck, she fell backward, offering her flesh to the older man. He laid her down on the luxurious seat of the car and brought her tiny butt up to the cushion as well. Sucking her neck, he lifted her skirt higher and higher until her panties were exposed. As the wealthy dad pushed up to his knees and looked at the naked slender hips and the bulge of the pussy of this young teaching assistant, his lust was more than his good sense could beat.

As Summer watched, Mr. Sandovar unzipped his pants and pulled out his amazingly large cock. It surprised and scared her but she was all his. He pulled down her panties to her ankles and removed them. He did not have to push her legs apart because she willingly spread them. When he lay between her legs, those skilled lips kissed her again, filling her with emotions and want to have him inside her.

There was no waiting. Suddenly young Summer arched back, feeling that big hard penis push into her.

"You are mine now, Summer."

He moaned as he buried the entire shaft in her, stretching the tight inner walls of her pussy. Without pause, he began to fuck in and out of her. His thrusts were more powerful than anything she had ever experienced, and she moaned and thrust back, letting her body take over to fuck him back.

In a sudden surge of excitement, the sexy

man thrust his cock deep inside of Summer and came.

When she felt his hot sperm shoot into her like it was coming out of a gun, it put her into orbit as well and Summer pushed up into his arms and orgasmed as they kissed.

The Sins Of Others

Summer was very worried for months after her exciting sex with that sexy dad. First, she worried about becoming pregnant. He filled her with cum and it was close to the time when she would have been ovulating. When her period came and went, then she had other anxieties. She felt so strange the next school day when she saw the little girl. Maria was a sweet little girl who naturally ran to Summer and hugged her each day she saw her. How could Summer forget the fact that she had fucked Maria's daddy?

More than anything, she worried about her job and her reputation. But as time went by and nothing happened, Summer simply vowed to be more careful and not be tempted like that again. She never spoke of the incident until after Maria was out of the school system and nobody knew about the Sandovars at all. When she did speak of it to her close friend Tina, Tina mentioned that it was good she changed her ways.

"You don't want to end up like Abby the Slut, do you?"

"Who is Abby the Slut?"

Summer wanted to know. This was a story that had become lore around the school. In reality, Abby was not a slut at all. She had been teaching at the junior high level of the school for ten years when the incident happened. She was respected by her students and the other teachers. She did not dress slutty or act that way. She was married with two kids of her own who were in elementary school. She dressed professionally and attractively in a way that accented her nice figure. She had a look that most people would call "lovely" rather than gorgeous or hot. But her smile lit up the room and she was universally loved.

The incident was not planned. It happened on a Thursday afternoon, which was like any other Thursday afternoon. Abby had sent a couple of kids to detention, including one particularly lippy boy named Jordon. Jordon seemed to think he could order his teacher around, and so the only way to establish her authority was to give him detention.

Because Jordon was in detention, he missed his bus so he called his brother Bryan to pick him up. Bryan was in junior college but he lived at home. He was 20 years old and he resembled a much more handsome, muscular, and masculine version of Jordon. Bryan did not know where detention was so he came to the classroom where Abby was cleaning up.

"Are you Mrs. Oberman?"

Bryan entered the room as if he owned it. His swagger and lack of shyness took Abby aback because she was used to dealing with junior high boys.

He went on.

"I am his brother, Bryan. They didn't have hot teachers like you when I went here," he said, entering the room and letting the door fall shut and click closed.

"Jordon is in detention, Bryan."

She was cold.

"He is in Room 222 and he should be getting out shortly so you can find him there."

Bryan crossed to her desk. He was standing right in front of it with only the desk between them.

"You put him in detention, didn't you? Why?"

"He was lippy and acted like he could order me around. That is ground for detention."

"Maybe he should order you around. There are some women that like that."

"I am not one of them," Abby said facing him directly.

"I think you are."

At that, he grabbed her wrists firmly and pulled her toward him. Abby did not have a chance to stop the boy before his mouth kissed hers hard and she felt his tongue penetrate her lips. Something in her responded and she kissed him back. He was so powerful and demanding that a part of her began to get very excited. When he finished the kiss, he put his other hand in her hair, grasping it like a handle so it hurt her.

"You kissed me back. You like being a slave to a real man. Maybe that cunt husband of yours doesn't know how to excite you."

He kissed her again.

"Stop, Bryan," she gasped but he didn't stop. Instead, he came around the desk and wrapped his arms around her from behind.

"If someone comes in, I will yell rape."

She moaned but her breathing was going wild and she found herself pushing back against him.

"But if they don't come in, I am going to fuck you, teacher woman."

"Oh God...," Abby gasped, but it was a sigh of passion, not fear or anger. Bryan took the sides of her blouse and yanked so the buttons flew off and he ripped it apart. He reached in and pulled down her bra so Abby's ample breasts were naked in her own classroom. Abby was terrified and turned on more than she had ever been.

Sensing her excitement, Bryan pulled up Abby's neatly pressed skirt over her hips and leaned over her body. Abby tried to struggle, but when Bryan held her firmly, she bent over for him, which only made her more excited. She felt his hand push down her panties to fuck her.

"No Bryan, please," she said, but as he felt into her slit, her wetness told him yes.

It was a blur to Abby as he unzipped his pants to take out his hard cock. As she looked out over the chairs of the students she taught, she felt that big cock drive into her and begin to fuck her right there in the school. Suddenly, almost without knowing it, Abby gasped, "Oh God, yes fuck me." That drove Bryan wild and he grasped her naked tits, squeezing them together and stroking the hard nipples, and fucked her in powerful thrusts. “I’m going to cum in you,” he moaned.

“No, not inside me!” Abby objected but it was too late. He buried his cock in her and filled her with cum. Just out of nowhere, Abby came too, falling forward on her face on the desk with her butt stuck up to take his sperm.

“Just then, the door opened and Principal Nightly stood there looking on at the filthy scene. Abby was renamed Abby the Slut and she was fired on the spot.”

Tina finished the story as Summer listened raptly.

“Wow,” Summer responded to the dramatic story. She vowed then and there to be very careful for as long as she worked at that school so she would never become known as Summer the Slut.

The Reunion

At 30, Summer was proud of her 10 years of teaching. Except for that one time with Mr. Sandovar, she had kept her nose clean. She was skilled at navigating the lustful stares of dads and 14-year-old boys as well. And she did so while still dressing like a girl in outfits that showed off her best side. She looked more like a 20-year-old new teacher than a seasoned 30-year-old teacher.

The first day of her 11th year went without incident. There was a good crop of students this year, and she had very little trouble from them. After classes were dismissed, she spent some time in the room getting it ready for a big teaching exercise she was planning for the next day.

As she was leaving, she saw Tina coming her way walking with a tall, slender, and very handsome young man. Tina spotted Summer and got excited. "Summer, just look who I ran into!" she squealed, gesturing to the boy who looked to be about 20 years old.

"Timmy?" Summer shouted with delight when she recognized him. When he nodded to her with a gorgeous smile, she just ran over and gave him a sweet hug.

"Miss Reynolds, Mrs. Johns, you both were my favorite teachers when I was here six years ago. God, that seems like forever," Timmy said happily in a sexy deep voice, but his eye contact stayed with Summer. When Summer looked over at Tina, Tina mouthed, "Oh my God," looking at the handsome boy. This brought a smile to Summer's face.

Suddenly Tina announced that she was late for meeting her husband and she scurried off. Tim and Summer laughed at her sudden departure. After an awkward moment, Tim said, "Well, why don't you let me buy you a drink and we can talk about old times."

"Oh, you are such a sweet boy. But I should not be drinking in a bar with a handsome former student. What would people say?" she said coyly.

"Well, let me see about that."

At that, he reached into the interior pocket of his jacket and produced a small bottle of rum.

"We could get some coke and share a little beverage in the teacher's lounge."

Summer looked around, and by this time, the school was quite abandoned. She agreed because she was enjoying his company so much.

Tim got a can of coke from the machine and it was cold. Summer used her security card to get them into the teacher's lounge. It was deserted and they could see the parking lot from the windows. It was also deserted. She got a couple of coffee cups out of the cabinet and some ice from the refrigerator, and they mixed the drinks.

"To my prettiest teacher ever." He toasted her and she just giggled. It felt strange to be so smitten with a boy 10 years younger than she was who used to sit in a chair in her classroom as a teenager. But he had become gorgeous and sexy in every possible way. They drank and chatted about silly things that happened the year he was in her class. Then he made his confession.

"Being here in school with you makes me remember what a huge crush I had on you in the ninth grade," he said, smiling. "I used to wish I could get a peek under your skirt and the idea sent me home to beat off about you constantly," he confessed, blushing.

Summer blushed deeply as well. She went to the counter to get a paper towel. "I used to love to call on you, Timmy. You were a delight to have in class," she said softly, her heart beating fast.

"Teacher, teacher, would you read us a

story?" Tim said playfully, waving his hand in the air.

"Anything for my favorite student."

Summer played along and she sat in a chair, pretending to open a book. When she sat in the chair, her cute skirt came up just over her knees. She pretended to read.

"Once upon a time, a very handsome former student came to visit his teacher and to give her a drink," she said giggling and she took a drink of her beverage. The alcohol was making her silly.

"Teacher, is this the one where Timmy wishes he could see up her skirt?"

Tim smiled impishly, staring at Summer's knees.

"It just might be that, Timmy."

She continued to pretend to read.

"And Timmy was always a good little boy, and it made Summer like him better than all the other boys in her class."

With her heart beating fast, Summer parted her legs so that Tim could gaze up her skirt.

It was a dream come true for Tim. He saw his favorite teacher's bare white thighs leading to her sweet cotton panties that clung to her sexy pussy just right. The view was dark because her skirt was over her legs, but it seemed that her pussy was a little wet, the lips of her cunt clinging to her panties.

Tim took a pen out of his jacket pocket and tossed it so it landed right at her feet. "Oh I'm sorry, teacher," he apologized playfully. "I think I dropped my pen." This made Summer laugh, looking down at that pen that was directly between her open legs. "Let me get it so I can take notes on your lecture."

Slipping out of his chair to the floor, Tim crawled on his hands and knees like a little boy would to Summer's knees. He put his hand on the pen but then he looked right up her skirt with his face directly next to her knees.

"I think the story should include how sexy Miss Summer looks right now."

"Oh Timmy."

Summer gasped but the alcohol and the very handsome boy got the better of her. As he moved his hands up her legs, he began to kiss her knees and then the soft skin of her legs just inside the lower thighs. "Oh my," she said in a whisper, feeling the wet softness of his lips on her thighs. At the same time, his hands moved up to her skirt and started pushing it up higher and higher on her legs.

"I think this is a story about how the handsome student seduced the innocent teacher," she said, breathing hard from her arousal.

"I think so too," Tim said and he leaned forward to kiss her mouth. Putting his right hand behind Summer's neck, he pulled her to him and kissed her deeply, opening his lips wide. The wetness of that kiss made Summer crazy, and she also opened her mouth so his tongue could press inside her lips to French kiss her deeply.

At the same time, Tim's other hand had

pushed her skirt all the way up to her hips. She had her legs wide open for her former student, and her panties were soaked, the wetness oozing from her cunt. Tim slid his hand into her panties and pushed the lips of her pussy open so he could explore the soft wet flesh of her pink slit. When he brushed her clit, Summer gasped and hugged his neck, kissing it.

"I want you so much," he moaned as he pulled her from her chair. "I wanted to fuck you when I was 14 and I want it even more now," he said, lowering her gently to the lush carpet of the teacher's lounge floor. The danger of fucking a former student on school grounds was the most remote thing from Summer's mind.

Kissing him deeply, Summer lifted her hips so he could slide her panties down her naked legs to reveal her wet pussy to him. Looking down at his beautiful sexy teacher, Tim unzipped his pants. The look in her eyes as he pushed his pants down and let his very hard cock out excited him tremendously. Leaning in over her, he kissed her and undid the buttons of her blouse. Summer was so eager to feel him inside her that she wiggled under him and found his hard cock with her hand. She gently explored it up and down and stroked his balls with her thin fingers.

Losing his gentle control, Tim pulled open her top so the rest of the buttons went flying. Summer reached in and undid the clasp in front of her bra so her small tits were freed to give to the sexy ex-student to taste. "Oh God Timmy. I want you in me," she said, softly lifting her hips and moving his hard cock into her slit.

As Tim's mouth closed over his teacher's nipple and began to suck, she aided him in fitting the tip of his big cock to her tight vaginal rim. Then she pushed up so the head pressed inside her, stretching the rim of her pussy as it did. "Oh God," Tim gasped, feeling the warmth and wetness of Summer's insides engulf his erection. He fell on her, supported by his elbows, and pushed harder. Summer kissed his neck and ear as inch after inch of his hard cock penetrated her deeply.

With one more thrust, Tim's full hard-on filled Summer's pussy hole entirely. His passion was exploding, and he began to fuck in and out of Summer, thrusting with the power of his hips deep into the soft parts of her insides. Summer held his neck and thrust back up to him, matching his powerful fucking moves thrust for thrust. Suddenly Summer orgasmed hard, moaning and pushing up, as her body was flooded with the overpowering feelings of her orgasm.

She was all his and continued to push up to offer him every inch of her cunt. Timmy began to fuck his teacher harder and harder. He pushed up on his arms and watched his hard cock come out of her, soaking wet from her pussy moisture, and then plunge back inside again and again and again. Then it hit him like a seizure and he came inside her, driving his cock to the balls to fill her with his cum. Strong eruptions of hot sperm shot out of his balls and filled Summer's womb with seed.

They lay in a pile for a while with Timmy inside of Summer, gasping and kissing. Finally, she kissed him and said, “I will probably get fired for this.” But she giggled instead of feeling bad about it.

“Well then I will have my middle school teacher all for myself.”

2 THE BASEBALL GAME

Josh was a good dad. When his son, Jimmy, got old enough, Josh got him involved in Junior Scouts. The program for the younger kids prepared them for the advanced programs that challenged the boys to become Pterodactyls, the highest order in the Junior Scouts. That achievement was so important that is could serve as a resume entry or to get favor on a college entrance application form.

Jimmy loved Junior Scouts because they got to wear uniforms, and the meetings were about fun and learning mixed together. The dads were encouraged to be the leaders of the "den" which was what they called a unit of 10–15 boys. Josh had been a scout too as a kid, so he had a lot of fun planning the meetings with the other dads and playing games with the boys

Everybody was enthusiastic about

planning a trip to the baseball game. Scranton had a pretty good minor league team and the city had built a nice stadium for the team, so it was almost like going to a big league game, except it was a lot easier to get tickets and the costs were manageable, too.

The day of the baseball game was a busy one. Josh and Jimmy arrived at the scout building behind the Catholic Church and got all the permission forms. People were coming and going everywhere, but Josh did a good job of identifying the boys and their adult guardian.

A big van pulled up and out hopped Calvin, one of Josh's best friends.

"Hey Calvin, is your dad coming to the game with us?"

"No, my sister Beth is. She is in college."

He pointed to the van so Josh could check Beth in as Calvin's adult.

As he approached, the window to the passenger side rolled down and a gorgeous girl smiled at him.

"Hi, I am Josh, Jimmy's dad."

"HI JOSH!" came the thunderous answer and then a volley of girlish giggling exploded from the van. As Josh looked into the window, he could tell it was filled with sexy young college girls all out to have a good time.

College Girls

Just then, the side door of the van opened and Josh was overwhelmed with the sight of four stunning and sexy girls all in very short skirts giggling and flirting with him.

"Now which of you is Beth?"

"That's me," the black-haired beauty in the front seat answered.

"Calvin did not say the Junior Scout leader was so sexy."

All the girls laughed. Josh felt soft fingers find his hands pulling him into the van. Just then, Beth opened the door, jumped out, and gave Josh a push. Josh was so surprised he fell into the van right in the lap of the girl next to the door.

Josh's face was between her legs, and she spread her sexy thighs letting the shocked dad get a peek up her tiny skirt at a thong that was barely covering her cute pussy.

"Amber, I like this soccer daddy."

The other girl in the back seat spoke in a low sexy voice. Josh heard the door close and he was inside the van rolling around a bevy of sexy legs and tits. He rolled over looking up at the luscious blonde behind the driver's seat just as Beth crawled between the seats and unzipped his pants

"Girls, I have to get back to the troop."

He moaned but he could not stop Beth from pulling his pants open and sliding his surprised cock out. It was already hard and ready to go when Beth's mouth found it kissing and licking the head. Josh looked up at the girl who had his head, and she stroked his lips just as the girl in the next seat put his fingers on her tit letting him squeeze it all he wanted to.

"He is so sexy, Suzanne. Let's let him meet Erin."

Just then, he was pushed to a sitting up position and looked into the back of the van. There lying on the floor of the van with her gorgeous legs open was a young girl. The other girls helped Josh to his hands and knees. Beth leaned forward and kissed Josh on the ear and bit it and whispered in a deep voice,

"Erin needs to lose her virginity to be in our sorority. You will be doing her a big favor. Fuck our sorority sister, Josh."

Erin looked up at Josh nervously. She never imagined she would give her cherry to a man who was a dad. She felt the pressure from the other girls and slowly pulled up her cute mini skirt. As Josh watched, the neatly trimmed pussy of the virgin came into view. Josh was confused and felt nervous about this. But his cock was rock hard and being offered the cunt of a beautiful virgin was more than he could resist.

He crawled on his hands and knees toward the coed. His pants were still on but his fly was open with his rock hard cock dangling out of it. Josh thought about taking off his pants, but he knew he had to be ready to get out of that van fast. As he got in position looking down into Erin's pretty eyes, he leaned down and kissed her mouth.

"I'm scared," she whispered to him. As he kissed her, he slipped his fingers into the soft folds of her pussy and pressed the lips open, so the pink hole of her vagina was revealed and ready to take his cock. Josh had never fucked anyone but his wife and this felt like a dream.

"I will be gentle."

Then he felt another set of fingers on his cock. It was Beth reaching in and helping the dangling cock find Erin's tunnel. He fit the head of his very stiff penis into Erin's tight hole. When Erin felt Josh's hard cock pushing to spread open her womanhood, she went off moaning and kissing Josh. This pushed Josh on, and he began moving and thrusting as her virgin opening spread open for him.

"Oh, God!"

As she said that, the head of Josh's hard cock entered her and stretched her insides. Josh gasped and kissed Erin on the neck and shoulder sucking and biting as his stiff prick pressed deeper and deeper into her. "Fuck me...," Erin moaned and Josh was unable to stop himself. He began thrusting in and out of the eighteen-year-old. He heard the moans of the other girls who could see Erin's pink cunt opened up and that hard cock fucking it deeply.

The van rocked as Josh fucked Erin harder and harder. He reached around and found the cool flesh of her ass cheeks, and held them tight to give him more power to fuck into her. Again and again, his erection filled her up, slid out covered with her pussy wet, and drilled into her again.

"I am going to cum!"

Josh moaned and just then, Erin had her orgasm. She gasped and clutched at the older man's shoulders convulsing in passion. That was all Josh needed and he buried his cock deep in the girl and shot stream after stream of his gooey sperm deep in her stretched out pussy hole.

Baseball Moms

Beth and Josh had to hurry once he finished inside of Erin. Josh had to get into the scouting building to help organize the activities before the departure for the baseball game with the boys. Beth let Suzanne drive the other girl's home in the van so she could be a helper and keep an eye on her brother.

"That was so hot. I want to fuck you so much," Beth said in low voice as the two of them approached the scouting building next to the church.

"Not a word," Josh snapped back. For the rest of the meeting, Josh had to force himself not to look at Calvin's sexy sister because each time he did, he started getting a hard-on about what happened back in that van, but he was a good dad and a good leader of the group and he kept his priorities right.

They had a huge group out with lots of little boys running around in their uniforms and both moms and dads coming along to be sponsors. Soon they got everybody into vans and caravanned to the ballpark. "Dad, can Stevie and his Mom ride with us?" Jimmy asked as everybody was loading up. Jimmy and Stevie were best of friends and Mrs. Franklin, Stevie's mom, was one of the best moms in the troop who was always there to pitch in and make each event a success.

"Sure Jimmy, pile in."

"Thanks, Mr. Seal."

"This is such a fun outing, Josh."

Ellen Franklin, Stevie's mom, got into the passenger seat. Josh was relieved to see Beth get into a van with other dads and kids but as she did, she caught his eye and they exchanged a knowing glance. Fortunately, Ellen did not see that enough to figure out the connection.

Josh enjoyed visiting with the parents as much as the kids. He and Ellen had a great chat on the way to the game. She was a delightful woman and easy on the eyes too. While not a beauty queen, she had a curvy figure, cute honey blond hair, and a magnetic smile. The Franklins lived just a few doors down from Josh and his family, so they were good friends in the neighbor sort of way.

Josh and Ellen sat together with Jimmy and Stevie in front of them so the boys could enjoy the game together. Josh found himself really liking this woman, and he was trying not to make eye contact with the sexy Beth who was seated not that far off. More and more, as he thought about fucking that virgin girl, he got turned on and then turned and talked to Ellen. Before long, he started "noticing" that Ellen had a great body. He even flirted with the cute mom a bit, and she did not seem to mind.

The night was a big success and it was over too fast. On the way back, Larry and his son Malcolm rode with Josh. His house was not too far out of the way, so Josh dropped Jimmy off because it was late and Josh had to clean up at the scout center. It took a while for all the cars to get back and everybody to get organized and headed on home. Josh got to work on the cleanup duties and was hardly getting started when he heard a car door slam.

"Need some help?"

It was Ellen. She had the same idea and after she got Stevie delivered to her husband, she came over to help out. Both of the leaders were sweaty from the night at the park, but they were good at cleanup and soon the place was looking much better.

"Whew, this is sweaty work. I hate to go home smelling bad."

"Well there is a unisex shower just down that hall for the church gym. Help yourself."

"I think I will," Ellen said with gratitude. "I have my swim stuff in the car so I have a towel and a change of clothes. Sure you don't mind?"

"Not at all."

He was somewhat aware as she walked by toward the shower. It just started to dawn on him that the shapely mom would be naked in there. Soon he heard the shower water start. He found himself hanging close to the short hallway that lead to the open door of that part of the bathroom complex.

Suddenly, he heard a yelp. Josh rushed toward the bathroom. "You ok Ellen?" he said entering the shower area.

"Spider, spider!" she gasped inside of the shower stall. Without thinking, Josh pulled off his shoe, pushed the shower curtain aside, and killed the spider. He knelt down, cleaned up the body of the insect with a piece of tissue, and threw it out of the shower stall.

"Oh my God! Thank you Josh. You are my hero."

He heard Ellen behind him as the warm water of the shower began to get Josh's clothing wet.

When he turned around both Ellen and Josh froze. He stared at the naked body of the sexy woman just a couple of feet away.

"Oh...," Ellen said pressing back against the shower wall. "Josh I...," she stammered very aware that the scout leader was staring without blinking at her ample naked breasts and the triangle of short pubic hair of her pussy. "I am so embarrassed...," she said awkwardly.

"Don't be," Josh said gathering his wits. "You are so beautiful," he said without thinking. When he stood up in the shower stall, Ellen saw the huge bulge in his pants caused by his erection. Her eyes went wide because even her husband had stopped getting that excited by her nudity.

"Are you turned on?" she said nervously.

"Very," Josh answered without thinking. "Are you turned on Ellen?"

"So much," She answered. "Don't tell Henry."

But Josh was not thinking about her husband, his good friend. His instincts took over and he stepped to the sexy mom and put his hands on her shoulders sliding them down her arms.

"You are so sexy," he said softly.

"You can kiss me if you want," she said as she reached down and touched the bulge in his pants. The kiss was urgent and messy because both knew it was a sinful thing they were doing. When Ellen felt his tongue enter her mouth, she sucked it eagerly. The passion was like she remembered her first years of marriage and had long forgotten. As she played with his bulging cock, the fire inside her thrilled her all over again.

"Do you want to fuck me?"

Josh was eagerly sucking her neck and shoulder and letting his fingers find her soft tits squeezing them and pinching them. His lust was rough and full of want. Ellen felt so alive. "Not here," She gasped as she turned off the water and left the shower stall carefully pulling Josh with her. There was a couch in an office across from the shower but they never made it that far.

Josh wrapped his arms around Ellen from behind, and kissed and sucked her neck pushing her forward. Ellen braced herself on the bathroom sink shelf letting Josh bend her forward. He was so demanding and lustful that she felt on fire with lust from being wanted so much.

"This is so wrong."

She moaned as he squeezed her nipples with the fingers of one hand and unzipped his pants to fuck her with the other.

"Take me, any way you want," she groaned in a low breathy voice. She arched her butt up to him as she heard his pants fall to the floor. Ellen was able to look back and see his hard cock arching up as Josh pushed her thighs apart and prepared to mount her.

"I am going to stick my cock in you, Ellen," Josh moaned biting her ear. He slid his hand down over the soft skin of her tummy and into her pussy, finding her clit and massaging it. As her pussy exploded with feelings from that, Ellen felt the head of Josh's hard cock slide along the slit of her cunt to find her vagina opening. It was soaking wet with desire and ready to be fucked.

Josh drove his hard cock into her in one thrust filling her insides with his big cock. He was much bigger than her husband and longer, so Ellen felt the cock in parts of her insides that had never been fucked before. Without a break, Josh wrapped his arms around her middle and started to fuck her in steady but lusty pace. Ellen felt so good being fucked hard for the first time in years. She bent her head back, kissed Josh passionately, and pushed back to his thrusting cock.

"Oh yes Josh. Fuck me deep and hard. I want it."

Ellen moaned out, amazed such dirty things were coming out of her mouth. As she said that Josh began to fuck in and out, in and out with animal fury.

"I'm cumming," he moaned and she did not even think about asking him to pull it out. Instead, she lifted her ass to him, and reached down and stroked her clit. As Josh exploded inside her deep hole filling it with cum, Ellen had the most intense orgasm of her life bending over and being fucked like an animal.

Discovered

Josh and Ellen were a mess. They were wet and cum was oozing out of Ellen's freshly fucked pussy. Josh left Ellen to finish cleaning up and change into the outfit she brought. Josh went into the small office that was opposite the shower area, closed the door, and changed into some gym clothes that he kept in his trunk as well. Then he sat down on the couch and thought about the amazing sex he just had with his wife's good friend and a cute mom of one of the boys in the troop.

He heard the shower kick in again meaning that Ellen wanted to wash the cum off of her that was oozing out of her filled pussy hole. Just thinking about how he had pumped his cum into an 18-year-old virgin and a sexy mom in one night got his erection going again. Just then, there was a knock on the door of the office and it opened a crack.

"Hi sexy," Josh heard the youthful voice. He looked up the gorgeous smiling face of Beth.

"I got worried about you cleaning up by yourself. That's a lie. It was so hot watching you fuck Erin before the game. I couldn't stay away."

Beth was wearing a short halter-top and no bra. She had on an amazingly sexy short white skirt that showed off her sexy brown thighs beautifully. If Josh had not had a hard-on, looking at the sensuous college girl did the job. He felt his heart about to explode in his chest as the sexy thing knelt down at his feet staring at the big bulge in his gym shorts.

"I couldn't forget your sexy cock, Mr. Seal," she said moving her hands up his legs.

"Oh God Beth, this is wrong!"

He moaned but made no attempt to stop her.

"Shh, our secret," she whispered but just then Josh heard the shower water stop. At the same time, Beth pulled his shorts down over his very stiff cock and his aching balls. His big erection sprung form the shorts sticking straight up in the air. As Beth wrapped her fingers around the shaft, she licked her lips making eye contact with him.

It was just as Beth leaned in and took the full head of Josh's cock in her mouth that the door quietly opened. Josh looked over at Ellen's shocked face. He had been caught. Just as Josh tried to say something to Ellen, Beth pressed her mouth over the shaft taking half of aching cock in her mouth and sucking it greedily. Tears running down his cheeks; Josh felt confused, worried, and very turned on all at the same time. He looked over at Ellen but she was not angry or emotional. As she watched the cock that just fucked her getting deeply sucked by a young girl, Ellen got very turned on.

Josh took a chance and waved Ellen in. She closed the door and slowly approached the erotic scene. Beth glanced up at Ellen but she was way too involved to stop sucking this gorgeous cock. Beth recognized Ellen as one of the adults in the troop. Ellen sat on the couch watching Josh's wet cock slide in and out of that gorgeous set of lips. Josh was so turned on that he wanted both women at the same time. He pulled Ellen to him and kissed her mouth deeply. At the same time he stroked Beth's hair encouraging her skilled sucks up and down the shaft of his cock.

Ellen was on fire all over again in a way she had not known since she was Beth's age. She reached into her shorts and panties and started to stroke her clit as Josh sucked her tongue in a deep sexual kiss. All of a sudden, Ellen felt another hand on her leg. She glanced down to see the slender fingers of the sexy college girl working their way up her thighs.

Ellen had never been touched by another woman before, but she was so out of control and she opened her legs wide to encourage the exploration. Beth got interested in the sexy mom kissing Josh that she stopped sucking him for a moment and moved both hands up Ellen's sexy legs. Then she found the edges of her shorts and slowly stripped them down pulling off her panties along the way.

"Oh my God!" Josh said softly seeing Beth pushing Ellen's legs apart revealing her sexy, freshly fucked pussy. Ellen watched as the gorgeous girl licked her way up her thighs and then lowered her mouth to her open cunt. As Ellen began to moan at the brand new feeling of being licked between the legs and the even more new feeling of it being another woman, Josh slipped off the couch and pushed off her shorts.

Josh knelt behind Beth and pushed up that cute skirt revealing her sweet round ass and the sexy bulge of her cute pussy already wet and ready to be fucked. Beth's ass was swaying as she tasted the pink slit of the mommy she was licking out. All morality was out the door as Josh stood and lay that skirt over Beth's back and lowered his rock hard cock to fuck the young girl. He parted her engorged pussy lips and found the sweet pink hole that was ready to be penetrated.

In seconds, Josh mounted Beth and moved the head of his cock to the opening to her insides. He thrust and buried his erection to the balls inside the girl. Beth arched up and moaned loudly feeling her horny cunt being filled with Josh's hard cock.

"Fuck her Josh. Do it."

Ellen moaned, out of her mind with desire. Josh wrapped his arms around Beth's slender waist and began to fuck inside her furiously. Beth's mouth returned to licking Ellen's clit and tasting the rim of her pussy hole that was oozing a mixture of Josh's cum and her own wetness.

The room was filled with sounds of slurping, moaning, and fucking. It was Ellen that orgasmed first holding Beth's head by the hair and arching up to it and cumming. Beth tasted an ooze of woman cum streaming out of Ellen and lapped it, and gasped at the feeling of Josh fucking her like a wild animal from behind. Within moments of Ellen's orgasm, both Josh and Beth came hard too and Beth fell forward on Ellen feeling the scout leader pump his third load of the day deep into Beth.

The three laid in a heap on the coach and floor. Beth kissed Ellen who kissed her back exploring girl love for the first time. Josh collapsed on the floor looking up at the ooze of cum coming out of Beth's vagina and running down her leg. Josh was aching from cumming so much and didn't think he could fuck another time. Just then, Ellen whispered into Beth's ear, "Now teach me to lick you out while Josh fucks me in the butt." That is when Josh new that this wild three way was nowhere near over.

3 TWO WOMEN

"You know Lindy, isn't it amazing we have been married to Tom and John so long and that we are so happy?" Gretchen said as she took a sip on her favorite Starbucks beverage. The two housewives enjoyed their weekly "girl time" at Starbucks each week.

Lindy had known her best friend Gretchen since middle school. Now in their thirties, they had shared all of life's adventures together. Their husbands, Tom and John were also best friends in high school, and the four of them double dated constantly. They had a double wedding so they shared the same anniversary date. Tom and John often golfed together or went camping with the kids, and Lindy and Gretchen enjoyed an occasional girl's trip just for them or with other women from their social circle or church.

"Yes, they are such great guys. We are lucky gals," Lindy responded.

"15 years is a long time," Gretchen continued, "They say the excitement goes out of a marriage after that long," She said whimsically.

"Well I suppose things do settle down a bit," Lindy said softly. "I mean you can't stay on your honeymoon forever," she said with a light chuckle.

Gretchen was the tall and elegant member of the friendship, and her long black hair was always perfectly in place for any occasion. She had that kind of classic beauty that made you think she came from royalty. She was very musical and taught piano or voice lessons. Everyone in church enjoyed her singing.

Lindy was also gorgeous but she was shorter and rounder. Gretchen often admired that it was Lindy that got the round figure with a full bust line, whereas Gretchen's breasts were small but a perfect fit to her slender frame.

"Do you ever miss the passion? I mean in the bedroom. Sure settling down is one thing but....." Gretchen asked.

"I know what you mean," Lindy said with sadness in her voice. "There are weeks when it doesn't happen at all. And when it does, it's like going through the motions. John almost always wants the lights off when we have sex."

"Tom, too," Gretchen said. "I worry about that. I mean I don't think our guys would ever have affairs but it makes you wonder.

Last month Tom went to that banking convention and some of the men that went got in trouble for seeing prostitutes. I am pretty sure Tom would never do that, but it gets your mind to wondering."

The girls knew to get a booth that provided them with privacy for this kind of discussion. They both blushed in front of each other talking about sexual favors that men want sometimes.

"I know men go to those women for things their wives would not do," Lindy said softly. "When we do have sex, it is usually in the dark, missionary, and its over in a few minutes," she whispered.

"I am the same way," Gretchen said. "But I would do those things for Tom to keep him from going to a prostitute or another woman," she confessed.

"Have you ever, you know, sucked it?" Lindy asked her friend.

"Oh God no! I know women who do that but I could never face the ladies club or go to church knowing I had been so slutty," Gretchen said with a nervous giggle.

"Gretchen," Lindy finally said after the topic had them both steamed up. "I think it is time to get slutty so we know for certain that our men never think for a second about going to some other woman for those slutty things," She said. "After all, if any woman is going to suck John or do any of that other stuff, it is going to be me."

Getting Slutty

The two good Christian moms and wives

made a pact that they would both try to be slutty to see if it will put some of that fire back in the sex side of their marriages. Gretchen decided to see if she could put Tom's penis in her mouth. She had never been face to face with it before. Of course, she had seen it as he got out of the shower and felt it going into her vagina during sex but that was about it.

She waited until the weekend and got the kids farmed out to sleepovers. Gretchen spent some time finding a cute short skirt outfit that would show off her legs well. As she strutted around admiring her shape in the mirror, a twinge of excitement got inside her at the idea of her sweet husband actually lusting after her.

She did not put on the outfit right away. When Tom got home from work, it was the usual peck on the cheek and then dinner. He settled into his chair to watch the news and that is when Gretchen slipped back to the bedroom and put on that sexy dress. It was white with red polka dots, and it was like someone a girl half her age would wear.

"Look what I found in the back of my closet," Gretchen said jokingly as she stepped into the living room and stood between Tom and his news show. Instantly, his eyes went wide when he saw his wife's sexy legs and how that dress showed off the curves of her hips and butt. Gretchen blushed when she saw him staring at her so lustfully. "Do you like?" she said turning and posing for him.

"Wow, sweetie!" Tom answered gasping. "I

had forgotten all about that dress. You still look amazing in it," He complimented her. The excitement he was showing reminded Gretchen of when they first got married, and she gave him her virginity. Tom was riveted watching his wife, and it was like he had forgotten how incredibly sexy she could be.

"Do you like my legs?" Gretchen teased her husband feeling bolder by the minute. She even pulled up her skirt a bit to give him a peek and felt naughty even though it was her husband after all.

"Baby, you are so sexy. What has gotten into you?" Tom said leaning forward in his chair. That is when Gretchen saw the huge lump in his pants.

"Let me be the boss lover," she said in a seductive voice. The good girl in her was shocked at how she was behaving but this was all so exciting. And she promised Lindy to take that one-step into being a slut for her husband.

Gretchen stood between Tom's legs and looked down at the huge bulge in his pants. She slowly lowered herself to her knees and began to massage his hard cock through his pants. "Oh god, Gretchen...." Tom gasped because she had never done these things to him before. Slowly she unzipped his pants. Part of her was terrified but most of her was aroused beyond belief.

Fumbling a bit because it was so new, Gretchen pulled her husband's fly apart and reached in and worked his underwear down. Then she found his very hard cock. Even when they had sex before, she could not remember it being this hard. It surprised her when she freed it from his pants, and it popped out sticking straight up from his trousers hard and arching back.

There was no stopping now. Leaning forward, Gretchen angled her husband's hard cock to her lips. She glanced at his face and he was stunned at the idea that she was about to put her lips to it. Gretchen looked at that big stiff cock of the man she loved, and then she did what she never thought she would do. She put it in her mouth.

"Oh God!" Tom gasped feeling his wife's mouth begin to suck his stiff cock. Not knowing how, Gretchen took as much as she could in her mouth and began to suck it like it was a lollipop. Soon Tom's hips began to move. Gretchen felt his hands gently holding her head and caressing her hair as his hips began to thrust that big cock into her mouth and out and back in.

Suddenly, Gretchen gasped around his hard cock as thick oozing fluid began to leak on to her tongue. It was too late stop. "Just a bit more, sweetie," Tom said in a low growl pushing his hard cock deeper inside her mouth to the opening to her throat. When he suddenly exploded, he heard his wife squeal with surprise. Cum shot out of his cock directly into her throat. Without even thinking about it, Gretchen swallowed the cum.

Comparing Notes

"Oh my God Gretchen," Lindy gasped hearing her story. "I did it to him when we were in bed. I thought he was going to have a heart attack when I put it in my mouth. He did shoot one spurt in my mouth but I got it out, and it shot all over my face and his legs," She said with a giggle.

"Did you have sex then?" Gretchen said keeping her voice down since they were in the Starbucks comparing notes.

"Yes!" Lindy said with enthusiasm. "It was the hottest sex we ever had! It was even better than our honeymoon."

"Oh same with us," Gretchen said with a happy little squeal. "I felt so dirty and wanted. I thought he would never stop climbing back on top of me!"

The two wives shared their adventures for quite some time and several refills of coffee. They had a lot to share because each couple had tried a lot of new things. Neither had tried any other position than missionary, and this experimentation brought in all kinds of new positions. Lindy had even had a short experience when her husband John licked her pussy and that was a whole new sensation.

"Here is something really new," Gretchen said softly. "The last time he was inside me. I was on top and he had has arms back there holding onto my butt cheeks and pushing hard" She said gasping because even the memory got her aroused. "Just then I felt his finger touched my rear end hole. I was shocked but I didn't stop him."

While anal play sounded gross to the two wives before this new era of excitement, Gretchen confessed that is was also arousing simply because it was so taboo. That brought into the discussion the ultimate taboo that Lindy had read some married men want. That taboo was sodomy with their wives.

Suddenly, the talk went quiet as Lindy and Gretchen thought about that. It was Lindy that broke the silence when she whispered, "I would give that to him rather than have him get that from a prostitute."

It was agreed. That would be the next taboo to try.

The Next Taboo

Lindy was very nervous about giving the last taboo to John. He had often remarked how sexy her ass was, especially since their sex life had gotten so creative. Since her last talk with Gretchen, Lindy had allowed John to mount her while she was on her hands and knees. The sheer animal excitement of being taken that way drove her into a new level of orgasm. But just as her husband was about to fill her pussy with cum, he grabbed her wide ass cheeks and pulled them open staring down at her puckered butt opening.

After he shot inside her, they spooned and he left his cock in his wife while it emptied into her cunt and slowly softened. He had become very attentive, kissing her back and neck and playing with his wife's large breasts happily. Then as she leaned back and kissed his mouth, he reached down and squeezed her butt cheeks.

"Do you like my butt sweetie?" she

whispered enjoying that feeling of being handled.

"Yours is the only butt that makes me so turned on." He answered in the darkness of their bedroom.

"I noticed just before you came, you spread it and looked. Did you like what you saw?" she asked. John took a few moments thinking about it because he knew she was talking about her anal opening.

"Yes Lindy," he confessed. "For some reason to me, that opening is very sexy."

"I know for some couples, the man goes inside that hole," she said thoughtfully.

"Yes," John answered tenderly stroking her skin. "I have thought about that especially lately."

"John," Lindy said softly. "I don't ever want you going to another woman for anything. If you want that, have it with me. I would give you that hole too. I belong to you."

John kissed her deeply and that was enough to tell her yes, he did want to have sex inside his wife's butt. Lindy had done some reading about it since she and Gretchen had discussed it. As she got the lubricant out of the nightstand, she wondered if Gretchen too was about to let Tom have sex inside her butt.

John slipped his arms around his naked wife in their bedroom. The kids seemed far away and they were fast asleep as their mommy and daddy prepared to do something new and taboo. As she felt his kisses and bites on her neck and shoulder,

Lindy pushed her butt back toward her husband.

She slipped the tube of lubricant into his hands and they kissed lovingly as he used both hands to apply the KY to his hard cock. Lindy even put some on it herself and as she rubbed up and down that stiff rod, she wondered if it could even fit in her anal tunnel. She pulled a pillow to her tits and rolled forward to give him full access to her butt cheeks.

"Go slow," she said with a tremor of nervousness in her voice. There was a soft light coming from the closet in the bedroom so John could see as he parted the ass cheeks of his beloved wife. Lustfully he stared at her puckered asshole. Then he took the tube and squirted a little lubricant on the tip of his finger. He slid his finger between the parted cheeks and began to rub it into the sensitive rim of her anal opening.

"Hold the cheeks open sweetie," he instructed his wife. Lindy obediently reached back, took one very white butt cheek in each hand, and pulled them open so the pink hole was exposed to John to prepare to penetrate it. Holding the shaft, he leaned in and fit the head into the rim of her anal opening.

Slowly John moved the head of his hard cock in the anal rim of his pretty wife. "It's going in baby," he whispered as he felt that hole begin to open for him. Her grunts of pain only excited him as he pushed gently but steadily to enter her butt hole.

About a mile away, Gretchen waited

naked on her bed to take her husband's hard cock up her ass too. He was in the bathroom bringing the lubricant. She lay on her back with her legs pulled up, so her butt was pushed up ready for him to fuck it. He entered the room stark naked with his long cock hard as a rock. She watched as he approached the bed while squirting the KY on his fingers and rubbing it up and down his hard cock.

"Are you sure you want this darling?" Tom said as he pushed her legs back so her shapely ass cheeks opened showing him her tiny puckered butt opening

"You deserve it," Gretchen said softly with some fear in her voice. "Nobody but you, sweetie."

Tom leaned in and kissed her mouth as he let his hard cock find the rim of her anus. She moaned and pushed up to him as he kissed and sucked her neck and began to push to penetrate her asshole. The position allowed Tom's pelvic bone to press onto her clit, and Gretchen pressed up passionately grinding on his crotch. "Oh yes darling, go inside my butt," she moaned as Tom began to thrust harder and harder. As her tight butt opening yielded, Gretchen gasped and pushed up and accepted her husband's hard cock inside that forbidden tunnel.

Something about laying on her tummy holding her butt cheeks open was so submissive and primitive that Lindy began to get very wet feeling the man she loved mount her ass. She slid her fingers to her clit and began to stroke it as she felt him pressing down on her. The father of her children wrapped his arms around her stomach and began to make humping thrusts to press his hard cock into her butt.

"I want inside your butt, baby," John moaned. It was so animal like and dirty that Lindy found a new lusty side to her husband. She liked this side. Suddenly, the rim of her butt seemed to open to him.

"Oh God, it's in me!" She gasped feeling the shaft stretch the narrow shaft of her ass opening and push deep inside her. He had put so much lubricant on his cock that it slid deeper and deeper without friction. Lindy pushed up as she felt his cock fill that hole going further inside her rectum.

Suddenly he stopped. She felt so full inside with all of his erection up her butt. "Do you want to do it to me now?" she whispered.

"Ask me to and I will, sweetie." He said kissing her back. She could feel how fast his heart was racing.

"Do it, baby," she finally said. "Fuck me in the ass!"

That was all it took. John pulled back and thrust inside his wife's tight butt hole and then again. At first, the thrusts in her rectum were slow because Lindy was grunting so much. Then it got faster and faster. Lindy pushed her butt up to him to fuck it, and he held her middle and fucked with more power like an animal inside his bride.

"Oh god, oh god, oh god. Oh god!" John gasped as he drove his rock hard cock into

Lindy's anal tunnel. He never imagined how exciting this could be. "I'm going to cum, baby," he moaned holding her tight to him and squeezing her big round tits in both hands. Almost as soon as he said that, John thrust his full erection deep into her rectum and the cum exploded into that canal. Lindy was stroking her clit with her fingers to match his thrusts. Feeling the hot surges of sperm filling her up deep in her ass put her over the edge and she orgasmed hard too.

The Boys Take Over

Little did the girls know when they began talking about this all that they would be allowing their husbands' sodomy. As they reviewed what happened, Gretchen confessed as well having an orgasm as Tom shot inside her butt just out of the sheer animal lust of it all. "Having him take me and make me his sex slave is so new and exciting," she told her best friend.

Tom and John could not ignore the big changes in their wives. They knew this was new and how close the women were. Things calmed down somewhat after the sodomy experiment, but for both couples, the bedroom was a hot place of passion again.

They got together as a foursome often and went to dinner. The girls could not help blush seeing the other's spouse knowing so much about what went on in the bedroom. What they did not know was that the boys had some plans of their own.

It was not too surprising when Tom and John were very romantic as they took their brides out together as a foursome. The romance was alive and well in both marriages since the girls seduced their husbands with forbidden love. The guys planned the night to put the girls in the mood. There was dinner at a fine restaurant and plenty of wine that was served without stopping. After the evening out, they retired to John and Lindy's house. They had a lovely living room that was lit in a romantic way with romantic music playing even before the couples entered.

The boys went to the kitchen to get more drinks, and the girls sat in the middle of the huge soft couch and whispered and giggled.

"You girls wouldn't be telling secrets now would you?" Tom said entering and that only made Gretchen and Lindy giggle more. Tom sat next to his beautiful wife on the couch and John did the same right next to Lindy as the girls faced each other. Almost like they planned it, the men slipped their arms around their wives and began to kiss their necks.

"You girls planned all those sexy things you did, didn't you?" John whispered biting Lindy's neck and sucking her earlobe.

"Yes," she confessed as both women were instantly swept away by the sexy kisses of their husbands. Gretchen leaned back and arched her face back to her husband who kissed her lips passionately. When she did open her eyes, she saw John squeezing Lindy's tits through her top and undoing the buttons of her blouse one by one. Tom saw Gretchen watching Lindy be felt up, and he unzipped his wife's dress and began to lower it down her top revealing the soft tan skin to Lindy and her husband to see.

"Lindy is so sexy, isn't she?" Tom whispered into Gretchen's ear. As he said that, John looked up and pulled Lindy's blouse open. He stripped it from her body leaving only her skimpy bra to hold her ample tits.

"Oh yes!" Gretchen gasped so turned on by what was going on. Both girls felt their hearts about to explode, as their husbands seemed to be taking them sexually right in front of each other. But their husbands had more on their minds than just fucking their wives. Just then, John reached over and took his wife's best friend's hand as Tom sucked her neck lustfully. John gently guided her fingers to the bra cup that was holding Lindy's left tit and he molded the finger around it.

Suddenly Lindy realized that the fingers on her boob were not her husband's. The girls made eye contact but their bodies were so turned on that they were unable to think about their objections. John released the bra strap and Lindy's bra fell down her arms. Suddenly Gretchen's fingers were on her best friend's naked tit, and she was beginning to explore her big round pink nipple that was already very hard from arousal.

"You are so turned on by Gretchen," John whispered in Lindys' ear and that suggestion created feelings in the two women that they could not resist.

"Oh God, John!" Lindy gasped putting her hand over her friend's on her tit and moving it around. "I am, I am!"

"Kiss her," Tom whispered to Gretchen and the men moved their slightly drunk wives closer and closer. Tom pulled Gretchen's dress down her arms and released her bra so both women leaned in topless. They could not stop the feelings their husbands had helped them get, and Gretchen lowered her mouth to Lindy's luscious lips and they kissed.

The boys were even more turned on than when they fucked their wives in the ass. As the girls made out feeling each other's tits, Tom and John scrambled out of their pants and underwear so their rock hard cocks were naked on that couch. Tom pulled up his wife's skirt and found her panties and began working them down so he could fuck her right in front of Lindy and John. John took Lindy's hand and put it on his cock, and as Lindy felt her sweet friend's tongue in her mouth, she began to stroke her husband's cock on that couch.

In one movement, Tom pulled Gretchen back to him pushing her thighs apart. John pulled Lindy on to the couch and yanked her skirt up to fuck her from behind also. The women saw each other's husband's hard cocks and realized they were going to be fucked in front of each other. That was when Tom slid his fingers into his wife's slit and opened it. The pink flesh was moist and inviting. John took Lindy's hand and moved it to Gretchen's cunt and she began to feel

Gretchen between her legs, finding her clit and then down to her vagina hole that was oozing with wetness.

John had gently but firmly pushed Lindy onto her tummy on the couch now parted her round thighs and opened the pouty lips of her rich pussy also. He leaned in and in one swift movement drove his cock inside is wife. At the same time, Tom from underneath his wife moved the head of his cock to her pussy hole and penetrated her as well. Lindy's fingers were right there and she slid those fingers down Tom's hard cock as her own husband began to fuck her from behind.

The women kissed again and then began to feel and suck each other's tits. The four became a jumble of flesh that could not be separated. John felt up Gretchen's tits and Tom slid his hand down to Lindy's cunt and stroked her clit as her husband was pumping in and out of her wet hole faster and faster.

Gretchen came first but that set them all off. Both women felt their lovers release huge surges of cum inside their full pussies. And that is when Lindy's came so hard she passed out for a while.

The shared sex was far from over. When they all got their faces, there was a lot of blushing going on. But before long, Lindy leaned in and kissed Gretchen.

"Wait, we are going to break this couch." The four horny friends swayed to the bedroom shedding what fragments of clothing were still on them. Inside that bedroom, every hole was fucked and every possible combination of sex had hours to be explored. The one thing all four knew for certain was that their friendships would never be the same.

4 THE HOLY MAN

The Journey

The wagon train slowly made its way across the prairie. It was a long way across the flat dry land in what would someday be Kansas. But not far ahead, they saw the landscape rising into the mountains. This particular wagon train was different because, along with cowboys and settlers, several members of the clergy are onboard. They were heading west to bring the gospel to the Indians.

In the lead wagon, a young nun rode along with the experienced cowboys on the journey. Her name was Sister Annabelle. She wore the traditional garb of her calling, a long black skirt and top that was buttoned to the neck and a small white collar. On her head, she wore a black bonnet with a white trim. She was far from the traditional image of a wise old woman serving as a nun. At 24, she was very young for the calling, but that is why the church leaders chose her and her brother for the journey. They felt young ministers would be better equipped for the rigors of the American Wild West.

Her brother did not ride in the lead wagon. She was there because there were more armed cowboys in the wagon and riding alongside for her protection. Father Lewis was in the last wagon on the train on that fateful day. He did not always ride there but he had made friends with a cowboy named Zeke and they liked to talk about religious issues. So their friendship made the time go faster. It had been a long journey, but they were making steady progress under the guidance of skilled and experienced cowboys.

Sister Annabelle had decided to sit next to the driver of the wagon for the fresh air for a while. Max handled the horses skillfully, and it did not escape him that the young nun was quite pretty and he could detect the hint of a lovely figure under those bulky gowns. He flirted gently but respectfully just as all of the cowboys treated both of their holy guests with all of the respect that was due to them.

Sister Annabelle was looking down at her sewing when she heard the hiss of an arrow and then the sickening thud. When she looked up, Max was grasping his chest that had a long arrow impaled into it. He groaned and fell off of the wagon dead.

Chaos broke out. Swarming from all around came what seemed to be an endless onslaught of Apache Indians on the attack. They attacked with flaming arrows and rifles that they had bought from traders or taken in battle. Annabelle screamed and fell back into the wagon. It was rocking back and forth as the horses cried out and bucked in terror. Flames from burning arrows burst on the wagon covering. The young nun looked around for the other cowboys, but they were all out of the wagon. As she scrambled to the back, she saw friend after friend fall with an arrow in his back, chest or head or from a gunshot.

Instinct kicked in. Annabelle dove out of the wagon and then under it briefly so as not to be seen by the Indians. She heard a scream as one of the young mothers in the wagon behind them was pulled onto a horse by an angry Indian who sped off with her leaving her small children to die.

Quickly, Annabelle looked for her horse, Rex. He had been tied to the wagon, and he was saddled for her and ready to go. He was a gift from her daddy when she was younger, and on Rex, she had learned to ride well before setting out on the journey. Just then, she saw her horse. He was free but he had not run because he was loyal to his mistress.

"REX" she shouted. The horse kicked back, and his back hooves struck an attacking Indian in the face knocking him to the ground. The horse needed no instruction. He ran to Annabelle and she skillfully swung up onto the saddle. Without a moment of hesitation, Rex bolted from the scene of death and destruction running like the wind toward some nearby hills.

Annabelle held on to his mane and whispered encouragement to her trusted steed. Then she looked back and saw two things that horrified her. She saw the wagon train engulfed in flames. She looked to the last wagon where her brother was riding and it too was on fire and she saw bodies lying everywhere. She feared deeply for his life. But before she could weep, she saw something else even worse. Two big, muscular Apache warriors were in hot pursuit and their steeds were closing fast on her.

"Run Rex, run!" she gasped hoping somehow she could outrun them.

The Outlaw

A shot rang out from the rifle that one of the Apache's was using. Annabelle was not hit, but she felt Rex begin to fall. He was hit in the back leg. When he began to fall, the Indians were on top of them. Another shot and Rex fell dead.

"NO!" Annabelle cried out seeing her beloved horse killed before her eyes, but the Indians gave her no time to grieve. She rolled over to see two huge and muscular brown-skinned savages pulling her onto her back. One of the Indians yanked Annabelle's long nuns skirt up to her waist. Suddenly, her thin white legs were exposed. That Apache fell to his knees and began to grope at her breasts through her gown.

Suddenly, the Indian gasped and his head

jerked back. Annabelle heard the gunshot after she saw the top of his head blow open. The other savage jumped to his feet scrambling for his rifle, but he was too slow. Another shot rang out and that Indian took a bullet to his heart. Both died instantly.

Annabelle pulled her garment down and struggled to her feet. She gasped and cried seeing the blood that was all over her skirt.

"Are you ok, Sister?" The voice came from behind. A man worked his way down the slope behind her and out of the brush. He was a white man, and he was dressed in rugged clothing, but he was well groomed. He held his rifle on his hip.

"Did you kill them?" she whimpered.

"Yep," he answered. "I can't have no savages raping a woman of the cloth." The white stranger said. Then he helped her gather her things together and called his horse. "Come with me. There are a lot of Apache around here. I can hide you."

He was respectful and gentle with Annabelle. When she asked if he was going to hurt her, he answered that he was raised Catholic before becoming an outlaw. So he held her position as a nun in great reverence.

"You are an outlaw?" she said softly when they got back to his camp.

"Tommy Frisco is my name, Sister." He introduced himself kissing her hand. "They call me the Frisco Kid. I rob banks."

"Sister Annabelle," she answered shyly. "You are no outlaw, Mr. Frisco," she said warmly. "You saved my life and that makes you a hero."

His camp was further back in the hills so it was safely away from the Indian activity. Annabelle was shocked what a civilized camp it was. Tommy went out, shot a rabbit, cleaned it, and cooked it for their dinner. After dinner, they talked and she found him gentle and understanding. She felt safe with him, but when she thought of her brother who may have died in the attack, she wept.

Tommy held her close as she wept petting her head. "He may not be dead. You escaped, so he may have as well," he said softly.

"I lived because of you, Mr. Frisco," she said looking into his eyes with her own large brown eyes. Frisco had never been this way with a woman before. He was a hard-living outlaw and mountain man, who only saw women when he bought whores in saloons. He felt a strange emotion of love as he cared for this gentle, holy woman. Without thinking, he kissed her lips.

"You can sleep in the tent tonight. I will guard you out here and sleep by the fire. Nothing will harm you, I promise," he assured his guest. Annabelle went into the tent and found blankets there to use and get comfortable. She slipped out of her skirt and top leaving her long undershirt and bloomers on.

Tommy sat by the fire trying to sort out his feelings, but suddenly, he was aware of the sound of a woman crying. "Sister Annabelle?" he shouted in panic and he dashed into the tent. The young nun had her face buried in the blanket weeping in fear. Tommy pulled her into a comforting hug, holding her close so the fears of a terrible day of murder and the possible loss of her brother would go down.

“Don’t leave me. I am so afraid.” She wept into his chest softly. Tommy slid down next to her kissing her forehead. He felt so many things, but along with caring and a close connection, he was aware he had the most beautiful women he had ever met all to himself in his tent in the woods. To become aroused for the young nun was sinful, but that only made it more exciting.

In the dark, she angled her face up to his and let him kiss her lips again. She had stirrings she did not understand and that the church did not allow. But the church and her brother and everything else were far away, and this sexy man who saved her life was right here. He kissed her deeply rubbing his hands up and down her arms. As his fingers wandered down her tummy, she let instinct take over and she moaned happily. His fingers slipped into her bloomers and found the soft hair of her sex that had never been touched.

Tommy was gentle in taking Annabelle’s virginity that night. He eased her bloomers off and kissed her neck and mouth as he stroked her pussy softly. Feeling it become wet, he eased her legs apart and pushed his rough clothing off. “I want to make you mine,” he whispered as he shifted between her legs with his cock stiffer than he had ever known it to be.

"I want to be yours, Mr. Frisco," Annabelle answered. Her body guided her to open her legs wide and lift her hips to take his hard penis inside her wet vagina. She moaned as he stretched her insides, but his kisses were exciting, loving, and full of his want for her. He slowly penetrated inch by inch to ease the pain and then eased it out and back in again. His fucking was patient and slow, letting both lovers enjoy every movement.

Before long, the urgency in both of their bodies took over. "Mr. Frisco!" Annabelle gasped as she felt what seemed like hundreds of tiny shocks go through her body. Her orgasm caused her to push her full pussy up to his eager cock and thrust wildly. That drove the cowboy into the most intense orgasm he ever had. His cock exploded inside of the sweet sexy nun's virgin pussy filling it with life giving seed.

Little did the two lovers know that they started their family that night. The Frisco Kid was an outlaw no more, and he broke camp the next day. Instead of going out to find a bank to rob, he joined his holy lover and went to make her his wife, and moved to New Mexico near a mission to the kind of Indians that threw them together that fateful day.

Father Lewis The Prisoner

Lewis did take comfort as the Indians swarmed around that burning wagon. He looked out from under the rubble and saw his sister, Annabelle riding away rapidly from the carnage. He knew that her horse, Rex as one of the fastest he had ever seen that somehow, God would take care of her.

Meanwhile all around him, his dear friends who were part of the mission, and the cowboys in the wagon train were being gunned down or slaughtered by the vicious Apache attack that was underway. He knew the wagon was going to fall on him and burn him so he dashed out from under it to face his doom. Instead of being shot with an arrow or a bullet, he felt a blow to the head and he went unconscious.

The Indian attack had been brutal, and all that did not escape were massacred—all but one. When Big Bear, the son of the chief, found Father Lewis unconscious on the ground, he knew from his exposure to white man culture that he was a holy man. He ordered his warriors not to kill the holy man for fear of angering his gods. They strapped him to a horse and took him back to the camp.

Chief White Eagle inspected the unconscious holy man and agreed with his son's assessment. He ordered that Father Lewis be put in a secured tent under guard. This was because he was still a white man, which meant the sentence of death remained on him, unless there's a reason to remove it. It was also to prevent him from being slaughtered by bloodthirsty braves who hated the white man with a passion.

Lewis woke up in that tent confused. He saw the fires outside the tent and the Indians dancing to celebrate their victory.

He decided that somehow, God had spared him to be a prisoner to these bloodthirsty savages and that he would try to find why God wanted him there. He would soon find out.

Lewis had sustained an injury to his right thigh. His pants were soaked with blood. Within hours after he woke up, the flap of the tent opened and a young squaw came in. She reminded Lewis of Annabelle because she was sweet, young, and had an innocent look to her face. She brought him food and water and her sweet smile was healing to his heart as well. She looked into his eyes and then placed her fingers between her small breasts and said softly, "Sashi." Lewis picked up on the communication and put his fingers on his chest and said, "Lewis."

Sashi then spotted his hurt leg. She gasped with concern and touched the wound just below the hip, which made Lewis gasp. Sashi's mother was the medical expert for the tribe so Sashi knew she had to clean and dress that wound. Touching Lewis's lips with her fingers to say do not cry out, she smiled and slipped away to get fresh dressings, water, and whisky to use to clean the wound.

Lewis looked at his priestly gown that was laying over a roughly made chair nearby. He supposed someone had taken it off of him when he was unconscious. He was glad to see it was not bloodied. He was nervous about the squaw dealing with his wound, but the pain was torturing him. When Sashi returned, she worked on his leg like a medical professional. She carefully cut away the fabric, which basically destroyed his trousers. The wound was several inches across, but it was not from a bullet. It probably happened when he fell on a sharp object in the confusion of the massacre.

But it was when Sashi removed the remnants of his pants that she gasped. The holy man's genitals were openly exposed to the young maiden squaw. Lewis did not have time to blush, as her soft hands were active in cleaning and dressing the wound. Before she bandaged it, she poured some kind of powder into the open part of the wound. Suddenly, the pain of the injury seemed to vanish, and that sensation was so powerful that Lewis moaned loudly and laid back sighing with relief.

They were alone in that solitary tent which was on the outskirts of the tribal encampment. Because he was wounded, the Apache's did not consider the holy man to be a threat, and if he had escaped, they were not prepared to stop him. He would not get far on that leg. Sashi gently caressed the dressings she had applied on his masculine leg. Of course, she had seen men in all stages of nudity as the Apache's were a natural people so they did not hide things from each other.

In fact, Sashi's garment was revealing, but it was a normal squaw outfit. It was a light one-piece buckskin dress that revealed much of her legs. This was for comfort so the squaws could work without a lot of fabric on them. But under that garment, squaws wore nothing so that they could take care of nature's business wherever in the country they needed to do so.

So Sashi had seen a penis before but never in such an intimate way. Her fingers were close to it, and she was without guilt as her fingers began to explore it and caress it. She heard the holy man sigh as he ran her soft fingers up to the head and back down.

"Do you like that?" she said in her own tongue, but of course, he could not understand that and she could not know what he said when he moaned "Oh yes." What she did notice was the rapid stiffening of the rod. Of course, Apache couples often make love in fields and young warriors and squaws watch and learn from that. So she knew that the hardness of his penis meant he wished to be inside a woman, in her vagina.

Sashi felt a new height of arousal greater than when she masturbated watching the couples fornicate in the fields. Having her hand on his hard cock made her tingle and want to be a woman to him. The holy man was confused feeling his cock so hard in the hands of this gorgeous dark-skinned angel. As he leaned forward, their eyes met and the affection in her eyes made him want her very much.

His morality told him not to fuck her. He had his vows to consider, and he could be killed for violating a tribal woman. But he felt he could be killed anyway, and while this was a sin, he wanted to be inside a woman once before he was gunned down by

Apaches or whatever way they were to execute him.

Lewis leaned forward captivated by her big brown eyes. As she played with his stiff cock, he kissed her. This was new to Sashi, but the feel of his lips and tongue excited her, and she learned to kiss back. She was still in a full squat position, which was one squaw women could maintain for days if needed.

Just then, Lewis looked down and saw her naked pussy between her gorgeous thighs. Then Sashi spoke in her own tongue. "Do you desire to go inside me?" she said, but he could not understand. But when she touched the tip of his cock and then reached up her skirt and touched the lips of her pussy, the message came across. He nodded his head unsure of how to go forward having never fucked a woman before.

Sashi was a virgin, but she knew what to do. She turned around and got on her hands and knees facing away from the holy man. Then she pulled her skirt up over her sexy butt and parted her thighs so he could see her pouty pussy lips easily. Looking back, she drew him to her gently until he was kneeling behind her. Nervously, he touched her butt and caressed it. As he leaned in, he felt her fingers touch his cock. The precious Indian woman reached through and found his stiff rod, and guided it to the lips of her cunt.

As soon as Lewis felt the warmth of her vagina rim, instinct kicked in. He leaned in, held her by the waist, and moved the hard end of his cock in that tiny hole. Slowly, her vagina rim opened, and in just a few moments, it let him inside. A deep moan came from the priest as he felt the warmth and wetness of her insides take his hard cock deeper and deeper.

Lewis was overwhelmed with emotions and began to fuck into her slowly so he could enjoy every thrust. He laid her on her back and entered her again. The sweet Sashi squaw looked back and kissed his mouth again. Her instincts responded, and she began to push back against his penetrations so they fucked in that little prisoner tent like one body moving together. It was only moments until Lewis's balls could not hold back, and he began to gasp and convulse pushing shot after shot of white man cum inside that innocent Indian woman.

The Minister To Virgins

Sashi came every day to care for the prisoner's wounds, and her stays went on for longer and longer. The tent was far enough away from the rest of the camp that the moans of passion were not noticed. Sashi and Lewis were both innocents to sex so they just explored what made them feel good. There was purity about it even when they fucked for hours, because to them, it was a gift from their different gods.

The glow that Sashi carried away from that tent was easy to see by the other women squaws. They didn't know it was the "freshly fucked" look but that is what it was. Before long, Sashi brought Aliai, and then

Naimi with her, and Lewis loved them too. There was no sense of sin, so when Sashi began to kiss with passion the mouth of her dear friend Naimi or lick the pussy of Aliai, to them it was just a new variation on a wonderful discovery. To them, they invented sex and they wanted to invent it all over again every day.

The braves of the tribe began to notice the flow of eager women squaws rushing to the tent of the pale holy man and how they came out hair out of place, clothing barely on and dripping from the pussy with the holy man's cum. The young Apaches knew the holy man was fucking their virgins and they plotted to kill him. They planned it during the big festival of the harvest that fall.

The tragedy that struck meant there would be no festival. The white man's army was on the hunt for the viscous Apaches that slaughtered the wagon train. Every Apache warrior in the tribe rode off to war the day before they had plotted to kill Lewis.

None returned. It was a total massacre. Suddenly, the tribe was reduced to old men and "virgins," and one very white holy man. The chieftains of the tribe met to grieve and plan how to find a way for the tribe to survive with all of their young men dead.

"We must kill the white holy man. We must cut him in pieces as a warning to the white man against this slaughter of our children," White Buffalo said sobbing over the loss of his sons and nephews. The chieftains agreed, and they brought Father

Lewis to the sacred fire to be killed. The chieftains stood in full robes for the ceremony.

Suddenly, Chief White Eagle sternly commanded, “STOP.” His eyes turned, so did the rest of the chieftains of the tribe. They watched as White Eagle’s oldest daughter Sashi casually walked by the ceremony carrying food for the chief’s dinner. The reason they stopped is it was clear to see the very noticeable bulge in her belly that was the result of a healthy baby growing inside her. That baby would be the start of a new tribe.

The death sentence was thrown out. “Father Lewis,” Grey Squirrel translated the words of the chief, “you must become the holy man for our tribe. From this day forward, you are an adopted Apache. You will teach us the ways of your god, and we will provide for you. You only have one other job,” the translator finished. “You will make babies in our virgins and start a new tribe from your seed.”

Lewis could hardly refuse. God had given him his calling to minister the gospel to the Apaches and to minister new life to the Apache virgins. One day the next spring, Lewis was swimming in a nearby river. Suddenly, he was pulled into the bushes. There looking at him was his sister Annabelle and her husband Tommy Frisco. The hugs and laughter they shared was healing.

“We are saving you from the savages,” Annabelle said. Just then, Sashi appeared smiling with her seven adorable babies running all around her.

"I am a savage too now Annabelle," he explained. "This is my bride, and these are my children." Then he gestured to the camp where babies and young moms were everywhere. "And those are my brides and all of those my babies too," he said with happiness.

"So you don't want us to save you?" Tommy said puzzled.

"No, I think I will be fine," the holy man answered.

5 THE PIZZA GUY

Prologue

Marriage was good for Alexis and Jeff at first. It seemed he wanted nothing more than to be with her whether it was to go out on a date or to just stay home and cuddle in front of the TV. Whatever the activity, it always ended in a passionate session of groping, kissing and fucking. Not only did this mean both of the married couple got their needs met but it made Alexis feel sexy and wanted.

She heard of marriages where the passion slipped away but she never thought it would happen to them. It wasn't children that caused it because they were going to wait a few years before having kids. But slowly, Jeff got interested in being with his friends and Alexis lost her skill for seducing him until he was so horny that being inside her was all he wanted. They still got along, but by the time they reached their fifth year of marriage, he seemed to like going bowling, playing cards, or watching sports with his friends more than being with his beautiful wife.

It wasn't that Alexis wasn't pretty. She had a look that many called cute or pixie-like. She had a round face although not fat. She worked out and kept her figure tight, and because she was not terribly tall, her 34B tits stood out well in her clothing or during the few times she was naked with her husband. When she was out shopping with her best friend Jamie, they enjoyed seeing heads turn to check them out. Of course, Jamie was nothing but sexy with her slender frame and cute tits. She looked like a model. But those stares that men sent their way were for both of them. Alexis could tell.

One of her favorite things was meeting Jamie at a local pub and enjoying drinks and gossip for the evening. She certainly deserved one night out with a friend as often as Jeff was away with his guy pals for night after night after night. The White Lion pub was a safe and friendly place so the girls got a booth and felt at ease there having a few glasses of wine. They were flirted with from time to time, but there was no harm in that and it made them feel pretty which is something their husbands failed at more often than not.

There was a small parking garage next to the pub that also served the shopping mall. Alexis said good night to Jamie and stumbled toward her car. She had a few more glasses of wine than usual so she felt nice. The drive home was only a few blocks on quiet streets so she felt she could drive and not have a problem.

Alexis got to her car and put her purse on the hood to look for her keys. Suddenly, she was aware of someone approaching from behind. At the same time, she felt sensations of fear and excitement. The attacker was on her suddenly. He pinned her on the hood of the car forcing her forward so she could not move. He was forceful and strong. Then he hiked her skirt up to fuck the pretty housewife.

Alexis was gasping and her heart was exploding at being handled so roughly. What surprised her more than anything though is that she became so turned on the more the rough man used her body for his pleasure. Suddenly, he bent her face back and she looked into the hard face of the attacker.

"I am going to fuck you hard woman." He hissed and at that, he pushed her panties down to the tops of her thighs. The horny man was unzipping his pants and did not hear that the words "Oh God yes" come out of Alexis before she knew the words were in her.

Suddenly, a police siren went off on an upper floor of the parking garage. It was for something else, but the man panicked and was gone as fast as he had come onto her. Alexis gathered her wits, pulled her clothing back into place, and got in the car. All the way home, she thought about what just happened and how much she wished that rough and violent man had been able to fuck her.

The Dream

Alexis did not tell Jeff or Jamie about the assault. But she thought about it almost non-stop. Her thoughts were not of dread but of desire to be taken by force like that again. If it happened again, she would only hope that the violent man would be able to finish what he started. She knew deep down that this was not a healthy way to view an attempted sexual assault. She never knew she had this submissive side inside her.

About a week after the near assault, Alexis was in bed with Jeff, and she could not get the assault out of her mind. Each time he thought of how he yanked her head back and how his hissed he was going to fuck her, she got wet and excited. As usual, her husband fell asleep without so much as a good night kiss much less a violent and needy fuck, which is what he wanted from him.

Slowly, Alexis drifted off into a fitful sleep. Suddenly in her dream world, she was at a college. She was a teacher at that college. In fact, Alexis did teach a few classes at the junior college in town several years back but did not keep it up. The dream had her back in those brightly lit halls pushing through the halls of excited junior college students. But in her dream self, she was her current age.

As she exited the building, she saw the football team working out on the field that was directly opposite the parking lot. The practice was over and the boys were running toward the dressing room, which was in the other direction. Just then, a big, muscular boy broke from the pack and ran towards her.

"Hello Mrs. Graves," the handsome football player said with a smile. He was a huge guy with a man's body, and he could easily overpower her if he wanted to. "You look very pretty today." He said and then he kept talking in haste as happens in dreams. "I have a crush on you so bad," he said blushing.

"That is sweet Danny." She answered him feeling her heart beating faster. "But I am married you know," she answered.

"I know you are Mrs. Graves," he said, and suddenly, there was as sinister sound to his voice. "Your husband is a shriveled up nothing, and I could crush him with one hand. He doesn't deserve you, but I do." He said in a threatening way that was scary and very exciting too. Just then, he was gone and the dream transported Alexis back to her classroom. It was about an hour later, and classes were out so she was cleaning up to get ready to go home.

Suddenly, the door opened and that big, muscular football player came in. He closed the door and walked directly toward Alexis in her dream.

"I want you Mrs. Graves," he said hungrily. "Right here and right now. I am going to fuck you."

"Danny no," she said with very little objection in her voice. Roughly, Danny grabbed her by the shoulders and lifted her to his face kissing her forcefully pushing his tongue into her mouth. When he finished, he pulled her to his body and walked holding her to him to her desk, which was empty from her cleaning. In one fast movement, he put her on her back on the desk and kissed her neck sucking and biting.

"Oh God Danny. It's so wrong. Oh yes!" she moaned as he pushed her skirt up above her hips. The dream woman version of Alexis was still cautious and she worried about someone walking in while Danny molested her. But there was no time for that. Danny was urgent to get his cock inside his teacher.

He rose up pulling off his shirt to reveal rippling masses of muscles. Then he forced Alexis' legs apart, grabbed her panties, and literally tore them from her hips. Her pussy was bare to the young freshman boy. It was oozing with wetness from the excitement of being taken without permission or talk. Danny just wanted Alexis, and it made her felt alive and sexy.

He fell on her tearing open her blouse and roughly sucking her nipples. It was Alexis herself that reached in and unzipped his pants. She pulled out his very hard cock and gasped because it was at least twice the size of her husband's. It was harder than she had ever known a cock to be even when she had her honeymoon.

As Danny entered her and began to fuck her, Alexis in her bed was moaning and writhing for real. She had worked her fingers into her panties and was masturbating to her dream as Jeff snored away next to her. In the dream, Danny drove his long hard cock deep into her and fucked her with powerful thrusts right on that teacher's desk.

"Take me, take me," was all the dream Alexis could say, and as her orgasm hit, both for real and in the dream, Danny came inside her filling her cunt with load after load of his cum. Just then, Alexis woke up soaked with sweat from the erotic dream. Her panties were also totally wet from her orgasm. She slipped out of bed, took a shower, and changed into clean dry night things. She slept in the guest room to be alone with her thoughts and dreams.

The Pizza Guy

These dreams came more and more often, and finally she confessed them to Jamie because she knew she would keep her confidence. Jamie was surprisingly understanding. She was married as well and knew that feeling of no longer being wanted when a man takes more interest in work or hobbies than in sex with his bride. Jamie also had a 4-year-old daughter and that took up much of her time and energies.

"I don't think there is anything wrong with you at all," Jamie told her friend. "When the men in your dreams take you forcefully, their want of your sex is the only thing that is driving them. You excite them so much that they just have to fuck you.

What woman doesn't want to be wanted that much?" Jamie comforted her friend. Finally, the girls agreed to put the topic to rest because even talking about it got them both stirred up.

Instead of having their bar night, Jamie and Alexis decided to just spend an evening at Alexis' house on Friday and watch chick flicks. Jamie's husband Paul was on the same bowling league with Jeff so the girls knew their husbands would be out until all hours drinking and playing poker after the bowling was done. Jamie got a sitter so they could take their time and enjoy their movie night.

It was a little late when the girls decided they wanted a pizza. They called their favorite pizza place and didn't worry about the cost or the calories because it was girl's night. Then they started watching Pretty Woman with Julia Roberts so they could swoon over Richard Gere. The movie made them forget they had ordered the pizza.

When the doorbell rang, the girls screamed like little girls but that was part of the fun. Alexis answered it, and the pizza guy came in through the door in the kitchen, got the pizza out of the carrier, and asked for the money. As she paid him, suddenly Alexis gasped.

"Wayne?" She said in happy surprise. "Wayne Jernigan?" She said. "Is that you? It's me Alexis Graves. We knew each other in middle school. I was Alexis Morgenstern then."

The big pizza guy smiled wide when he

recognized the pretty girl he knew so many years ago. "Alexis!" he said and they hugged.

"Jamie, look who the pizza guy is!" Alexis shouted, and when Jamie came in, she recognized him too. It turned out that he owned the pizza place and was about to close up when their order came. So he had to deliver it himself.

"And look who it is!" he said laughing. "The two cutest girls in middle school is all."

Both girls giggled at the compliment. Then they talked Wayne into having a beer with them. He had closed up the pizza place so he didn't have to run off. They spent some time catching up. Wayne was divorced for several years, but he had a girlfriend who was not someone Alexis or Jamie knew. Wayne knew Jeff also from school, and he made Alexis promise to say hi to his old friend.

The girls said a fond goodbye to Wayne, took the pizza into the big living room, and put it on the table in front of the wide couch they were laying on. But as they watched, they became aware that Wayne had wandered in and was watching the movie too. Finally, Jamie giggled and turned to him.

"Wayne you goof, if you want to hang out and have some pizza with us, it's fine," she said happily and he took seat in a soft chair. But his eyes were on the girls as much as it was on the screen. He was staring without shame at Alexis more than anything else in the room.

After about a half hour, Jamie's cell

phone rang. She excused herself, as the babysitter was not feeling well so she had to leave. Both Wayne and Alexis wished her well, but Wayne made it very clear he was staying. "You don't have to hang around if you don't want to," Alexis said feeling awkward.

"Oh I want to," he said with an emphasis on the word "want." The house was quiet except for the movie, which had continued to play while they said goodbye to Jamie. Alexis and Wayne both got another beer. She felt a little strange being alone with another man, and the way he looked at her face and body was a little scary. But it also made Alexis feel desirable which was exciting to her.

"I am so glad to see you again." Wayne said softly as the credits of the movie rolled.

"Me too," Alexis answered. "You were like my best friend in middle school."

"Well I can tell you this now Alexis that I always had a bit of a crush on you," he answered smiling and blushing. Alexis felt her blush explode on her face too.

"I don't know what to say Wayne," she said flustered. "I am married now of course," she said to try and slow things down.

"I know," he said moving closer to her on the couch. "But he isn't with his beautiful and sexy wife tonight is he? I am and I always dreamed what it would be like to kiss you." Even Wayne was shocked at how bold he was being. He felt very turned on being alone with the girl he had beat off to so often when he was a teenager. While they were both older, she was still amazingly sexy to him.

Alexis became very aware of her outfit as Wayne looked at her with obvious lust. She was wearing a loose t-shirt with no bra and a cute pair of shorts. It was not a dressy outfit because she thought she was just hanging out with Jamie all night long. But it showed off her sexy legs very well, and Wayne was clearly getting turned on looking at the married woman's exposed thighs.

Wayne moved closer and closer. "I am going to kiss you Alexis," he said in a low voice.

"Please don't Wayne," she protested weakly but he wasn't asking. The more Wayne leaned in, the more Alexis leaned back until she was laying on the pillows of the couch looking up at him. She knew that while she was protesting, her gaze of want and excitement told Wayne all he needed to know. As he leaned in for that kiss, Alexis turned her face away a little so maybe he would just kiss her cheek.

Instead, Wayne took her face in her hands and moved it toward his own. He pushed his lips on hers and kissed her hard. This was no friendship kiss. That action of forcing that kiss only excited that part of Alexis that wanted to be taken by a lustful man. She opened her lips and kissed him back. That only excited Wayne even more because he felt her desire.

"Please Wayne, stop," Alexis gasped when he stopped kissing her mouth. But instead, he just started kissing her neck and his arms slipped around her rubbing her back. Wayne felt Alexis pushing up to him and breathing deeply so she was clearly turned on by what he was doing. A demanding side of him came out the longer it went on. This was especially true as she responded with excitement to the force he was using.

Wayne slid his hand through Alexis' hair, caressing it as he sucked her earlobe. But then he felt a surge of want and he pulled her head back by the hair and sucked her neck and shoulder. He even bit her shoulder, which caused Alexis to cry out in pain and pleasure and push up to him. "Oh Wayne," she gasped feeling his teeth and mouth on her flesh. "This is so wrong. My husband...." She tried to say, but he just kissed her forcefully pushing his tongue deep in her mouth at the same time.

Alexis could feel the pressure of Wayne's erection through his clothes as he laid on top of her on the couch. Sucking and kissing her neck, Wayne pushed his hand under her top, found her naked tit, began to stroke, and squeeze it. "I always wanted to feel your tits," he whispered, as he found her nipples hard and turned on to his touch. Suddenly, Alexis was aware that Wayne's other hand was between their hips.

Wayne unzipped his pants to get his rock hard cock out to fuck his best friend from school. When Alexis realized he was pushing his pants down still on top of her and feeling her tits, her mind went crazy and she felt overwhelmed. She was cheating on her husband but in a way, she was being taken against her will. She had this fantasy of being taken but she never thought it would be this way. It was so much more intense and exciting than she ever imagined.

"I am going to fuck you," Wayne said when his cock was out and pressing against her stomach. Immediately, he began working her shorts down her hips and the bulge of her pussy began to emerge. Wayne kissed Alexis on the lips hard running his hand slowly down her tummy and into the soft bush of her cunt. Alexis kept her hair trim so she looked good in a bikini or sheer panties but she did not shave. Since until now only Jeff ever saw her pussy and he didn't care, it just wasn't worth it.

Suddenly, Alexis had a wave of guilt. She had never cheated on Jeff before, and despite his faults, he was still her husband. "No Wayne, please," she gasped pushing his arms up. But Wayne slid his fingers into her slit and felt the wetness in her pussy so he knew Alexis was turned on by being dominated. He grabbed her hands and pinned them to her sides. He shoved them under her back and pressed down so her own weight pinned her arms.

In one jerk, Wayne grabbed the top of Alexis' t-shirt and ripped it down. The fabric tore causing Alexis to gasp and scream a little bit. Roughly, Wayne dropped his mouth onto her left tit and began to suck it hard. "Oh god!" Alexis cried out feeling her nipple pulled deeply into his mouth and that hard sucking action. It was so intense that she moaned in pleasure and pain. The two

and deeper until it filled up her hole.

Wayne pushed up and looked down to watch his hard cock come out of her insides all wet with her pussy juice. They he drove it back into her again and again. With her arms free, Alexis reached up and pulled Wayne on top of her hugging his neck as he pumped in and out of her cunt. "Oh fuck me," she moaned now forgetting about any reservations about becoming the sex property of her molester.

Wayne thrust deep into her wet pussy filling it up and then pulling out only to fill it again. He wanted to memorize the feeling of her warm insides sucking on his cock as he fucked her so he never forgot this moment. "Oh God Alexis, I always wanted you." He moaned as he grasped her butt cheeks and began to slam into her harder and harder. Alexis lifted her thighs, angled her pussy so he could drive as deep as he could, and fucked up to him.

Their lips locked in a deep and sexy kiss. Alexis sucked his mouth hungrily feeling new highs of excitement she never ever felt with her husband. Wayne's big cock filled and stretched her pussy and went deeper into her hole than Jeff ever got. Both lovers grunted in unison and his cock drove into her, then drove in, and then drove in again.

"Oh God!" Wayne shouted when his orgasm hit him like a freight train. He doubled over into the breasts his middle school best friend and his back muscles drove with all the force they had to push his cumming cock deep into her. With his cock buried in Alexis to the balls, he started to cum. The surges of hot sperm shot out of him and filled up the married woman. Alexis came again as she felt that surge of hot cum inside her and kissed him holding him deep in her womb.

It took a long time for the stream of cum to stop filling up the happy housewife. She had sinned and it was good. She had cheated and she was never so happy. She had been seduced. The only thing she feared about being taken like a sex slave was one thing. She worried that it would never happen again. But she knew as long as she knew the number for the pizza guy and Jeff kept having nights out with the boys that Alexis was going to get seduced over and over again by that sexy pizza man.

6 ACCIDENTAL VAMPIRE

Prologue

Barclay waited patiently for his class in literature at the New England Junior College to get started. He had been teaching at the school as an adjunct for three years and he enjoyed it a great deal. Not only did it put a little extra cash in his bank account, but also it gave him a chance to lead his classes in stimulating discussions about the great books of English literature. Since he was the professor, he got to pick the books.

The class filled up quickly. Barclay was a popular teacher and this session was always one of the most popular of the curriculum. He had assigned the class to read Dracula by Bram Stoker. College students could not get enough of the legend of the greatest vampire of all time. The discussion period was fun and exciting, and the longer they talked about the vampire, the more stirred up some of the students became. It was impossible not to notice that the students that got the most into the discussion were the cute college girls that filled his classroom each day.

Barclay was engaged to a gorgeous girl whom he adored. Julia was a tall and slender beauty with perfect curves that looked as sexy in clothes as out of them. Her long black hair was outrageously sexy. At 24, she was ten years younger than Barclay and she was a wild cat in bed as well. Anyone who saw Julia and Barclay together when they were out was amazed that such a plain-looking man could get such a hot woman to marry him.

With such a sexy woman to be inside every night if he wanted, it shocked Barclay that he felt tempted by the cute college girls that came to his classes. On the day of the Dracula discussion, the three co-eds that sat on the front row seemed to ooze sex in his direction. Kimberly, Savannah, and Suzanne loved Barclay's class, and it was impossible for Barclay to miss that all three girls were wiggling in their chairs as they spoke of the dangerous vampire, Nosferatu or Dracula.

When Barclay saw how the three gorgeous 19-year-olds seemed almost turned on, he focused the discussion more on the appeal of the vampire. The more turned on the girls got, the more they wiggled and those sexy legs opened, giving him great peeks up their short skirts. Before long Barclay had to stand with a clipboard in front of his pants because of the hard-on he had looking at those sexy panties.

Professor Duncan

Barclay walked briskly back to his office after class. He was pretty sure he was going to have to close the door and masturbate after seeing all those sexy thighs and barely concealed pussies in class. Before he got there, he heard giggling coming out of one of the offices. As he approached, he saw coeds crowding to get in to see Professor Duncan. Barclay was a good friend with John, so his curiosity was excited, especially after staring lustfully at the three gorgeous freshman girls from his literature class.

When he got a peek, the college girls were all over John Duncan as he sat in his chair in his office. One was seated on his desk with her legs up on the chair so he could see right up her skirt. He was rubbing her thighs and moving his fingers up toward her pussy as a second beautiful redhead kissed his neck and pushed her hand under his shirt. Just then, John spotted his friend and laughed. "Oh, hi, Barclay," he said loudly. Quickly the girls got themselves together. John had the girls excuse themselves while he talked to his good friend.

"That was quite a harem you had there, Mr. Duncan," Barclay said.

"Well, I have magnetism for coeds. It is somewhat new," John said. "These girls have good reason to want more of me," he said mysteriously.

"I just left teaching some sexy coeds

about Dracula and I never seen girls in a classroom that turned on," Barclay told his friend.

"Oh there is a good reason for that," John said. "Why don't you meet me at the park this evening and I will fill you in," he went on. By this time, Barclay was very interested in all of this mystery. "See you then. I have student advisory meetings all afternoon," John finished as he vanished back into his office.

"Professor Duncan, your 4:30 is here," the intercom in John's office announced.

"Send her in, Betty," the professor answered, getting out the paperwork for the next student who had an appointment. This was the time of the year that each student met with his or her advisor to plan out their next semester's classes and to be sure they were on track to get their degree as planned. John opened the portfolio and gasped at the picture of the sweet and adorable girl that was about to walk into his office. "Ashley Matthews," he said in a low tone and suddenly he felt that "hungry" sensation from deep within him.

The young girl knocked on her advisor's door and he called for her to come in. She was an absolute doll. Her long blond hair was straight and simple, flowing down over her tiny shoulders. She wore a cute dress with a belt. The top had big red buttons barely containing her large breasts. The skirt came to just below her panties when she sat down nervously in front of the desk of her professor. John felt that hunger in him grow rapidly. It was a new hunger he had given into more and more since that visit to the cave a few weeks before.

John picked up Ashley's folder and moved to the couch next to his desk. "Let's go over your enrolment options," he said, but already his voice was getting deeper and smokier as it did when he made the change. Ashley felt nervous, and something like fire in her stomach began to burn. There was a draw to this middle-aged professor that was more powerful than what she had ever felt for a boy. She was confused and aroused all at once.

Professor Duncan tried to look at the paperwork, but instead his eyes were drawn to those sexy thighs right next to him. "You are a beautiful girl, Ashley," he heard his husky voice saying. Ashley knew this was out of line for a professor to say to her. But her breathing was labored, her brow sweating, and she was wigging from arousal just from being next to this man. There was something very animal about it.

"Professor Duncan, you are my dad's age," she said weakly.

"But I am not him," she heard the low growl answer, and when he turned his face to meet hers, there was a red glow in his eyes. The professor pulled the young girl to him and kissed her hungrily. Before his lips found hers, all she could get out was a slight "oh" and then she was his to take.

Ashley was overwhelmed with the feeling of desire that was coming from the powerful creature. The professor sucked her neck hungrily, and those fangs that came out when he was full of hunger began to sharpen. He did not sink into the flesh just yet. Instead, he pushed her back onto the couch, pulling her tiny skirt up over her cute panties.

"Oh Professor, take me," she gasped out of control with desire. It was as if another worldly force has taken her over and made her want nothing more than to be fucked and completely consumed by this wild animal of a man. By instinct, the young college girl opened her soft thighs as wide as she could as she felt Professor Duncan climb between her legs. His strong hand closed over the top of her panties, and in one rip, he tore them from her body.

The professor pushed up, gazing at the beautiful coed as if she was food. She was both terrified and more turned on than she had ever felt in her life. When she looked into those red eyes, which have full of lust to fuck her, Ashley orgasmed hard. The orgasm took her over and she writhed on the couch as the hungry vampire ripped her blouse open, causing the buttons to fly all over the room. Then he yanked on her white bra and it tore away, revealing the soft white flesh of Ashley's amble tits.

Ashley barely came out of her swoon when the big professor fell on her as he pulled his rock-hard cock from his pants. Instinctively she thrust up to him and the hard missile found its mark. He drove into her up to the balls in one thrust. As Ashley arched back to cry out, the professor's hungry mouth kissed her, muffling her moans of pain and ecstasy. His tongue thrust into her mouth even as his hard cock fucked in and out of her pussy hole.

Without a pause, Professor Duncan lowered his mouth to those sweet nipples that pushed up to him. He sucked the right one hard as his hands pulled Ashley's pussy up for him to fuck her deeper. Those fangs were sharp and ready, and they sank into the flesh of the sweet young girl just next to the nipple of her right breast. The pain caused Ashley to moan out and fuck up to the vampire wildly. As her blood flowed into his mouth and he swallowed it, the professor suddenly buried his hard cock as deep as it would go. He came in her as she orgasmed again and passed out from the pure pleasure of becoming his sexual property and food.

The Cave

Barclay saw his friend John approaching the park around dusk. As soon as John sat down on the bench, he got right to the point. "I have something to show you that will clear up the vampire mystery we were talking about before. Come on," he said and the two got up and started walking west toward the wilder edges of the park.

"I was surprised how aroused the girls in my class got just talking about Dracula," Barclay recalled. "I have never seen that reaction to a reading assignment before."

"It is more than a reading assignment to them," John explained. "Girls between the ages of 18 and 25 instinctively become aroused and drawn to the vampire. It is primal. They cannot help it. They can smell a vampire in their midst and they will gravitate to him. If the beast demands blood, they give in with excitement. It is both animal and sexual," he explained.

"That doesn't sound like the movie vampires I have seen," Barclay responded.

"Those movies clean up the vampire reality. Most of what is in those movies is bullshit. That is especially true of the ones we have now where the vampire is a sensitive soul. The vampire is a blood-seeking animal who cannot resist his need for the blood and pussy of young girls. The vampire is always male, and the idea that the bite of a human vampire will turn you into one is also bullshit."

"When a young girl is ravished by a vampire and he takes her blood, she does not become a vampire. But her sexuality explodes and she develops a deep need to give herself to a vampire again and be fucked by him. The orgasms she has from his attack are so powerful that they can never be reproduced by a human male. That is why you saw so many young girls hanging around my office today. They wanted more. They wanted me to feed their blood."

Suddenly Barclay understood what his friend was saying. "John, do I need to be afraid right now?" Barclay said with some tremor in his voice.

"No," John said warmly. "Vampires do not attack men. They also do not take girls under the age of 18. That is not about morality because vampires have no morality. It is just that only girls 18–25 have blood that can satisfy us," he said as they entered the mouth of a very large cave. "You do not have to worry about me turning you into a vampire. I could not do that. There is only one way to have that to happen," he said as Barclay used his flashlight to move into the cave deeper. "That is by a bat."

"What do you mean by a bat?" Barclay asked, spinning around. But his friend John was gone as though he disappeared into thin air. Suddenly Barclay heard the flutter of wings. The huge bat hit his head first and he fell back and got hit on the stonewall. As soon as he fell to the cave floor, he was unconscious.

What Have I Become?

The first thing Barclay was aware of when he woke up was the weight on his hand. He moved it and there was a flutter of wings of a very large creature. The bat lifted off of his wrist where it had been feeding, and it flew away. Barclay pulled his arm up and saw the blood coming out from a very large gash in his vein. Oddly though, as soon as the bat released him, the wound closed up and the bleeding stopped.

Barclay stumbled out of the cave, confused and disoriented. The idea that he was a vampire was terrifying because it brought up all of the terrible images from really scary vampire movies. As he ran along trying to find civilization to get to feeling normal again, he saw a sorority house ahead. He stumbled out of the dark into the light of the parking lot and stopped to catch his breath.

"Mr. Rogers?" a sweet female voice hit his ears. He turned toward the voice; it was Savannah from his literature class. She was a very sweet girl. She had a petite look about her. Her face was angelic, especially with her short hair curling under her chin like it did that night. "Are you ok?" she asked, rushing to him. She got to him and held his arm until he could sit on a bench in front of the sorority house where she lived. "Oh my God, you are hurt!" she gasped when she saw the blood on his shirt where the bat had bit him and the bump on his head.

Sweet girl Savannah escorted him to her room in the quiet sorority house. Little did she know she was inviting a vampire into her bedroom. As Barclay sat on her bed, he began to get his human wits about him and felt better. Savannah was in her bathroom washing her face, and he caught a view of her from the side. Her cute breasts were shaped in her shirt perfectly, and her butt was nicely rounded in her skirt. The jean skirt was cut midway down the thigh, showing off Savannah's smooth white legs.

"That was such a great discussion about Dracula today, Mr. Rogers," the pretty coed said from the bathroom. "I don't know why, but it was really kinda exciting to think of what if there really were vampires in the world," she said with a giggle. Suddenly that cute giggle woke something up inside of the college teacher. When the sweet girl entered the room with that gorgeous smile on her face, he felt this primal hunger just show up in his deepest places.

It was hunger but not just a simple kind like he had for a meal. It was hunger to become one with Savannah. It was hunger to own her...to drink from her bloodstream... to be inside her. It was lust but more than just horniness. It was a deep need to fuck her that he felt he had to satisfy or he would perish.

"I was just telling Suzanne and Kimberly that you are my favorite teacher, Mr. Rogers," Savannah chattered happily, as she came out of the bathroom. But when she looked at her teacher, she froze. While nothing on the outside had changed, a powerful magnetism was coming from him. Instantly her pussy became wet and she felt a want for him that she could not explain or resist.

"Oh my God," the girl gasped in a low whisper. "What is happening?" she said with a mixture of fear and lust in her voice. As she watched, her sweet teacher's eyes developed a red glow.

"Savannah, I can't stop this," he said and his voice had descended to a deep growl like an animal. "I am going to fuck you," he said and the low growl that came from his voice was alien to him. *What have I become?* he thought to himself with the rational mind that was now just an observer to what the lustful vampire was about to do to this sweet innocent college girl.

"Oh God yes. Take me," Savannah said as she felt her soul go under the spell of the creature that had taken over her professor. Suddenly that other worldly voice of the vampire and the surge of sexual attraction that washed over the girl got to her, and she orgasmed, still in her clothing. Barclay watched in amazement as it seemed like her body was hit with an invisible tidal wave. That only made his lust for the body of young Savannah even more urgent. But the human inside him saw her begin to fall, and he sprang across the room in one leap and caught her by her armpits. He picked her up in his strong arms, carrying her like a baby.

Savannah woke up in the arms of the vampire. His red eyes glowed with a weird combination of lust and concern. But the lust was winning. When he smiled, the gleam of his white fangs sent chills of fear and excitement through her. Instantly she was aroused again and she leaned up to his handsome but sinister face. They kissed deeply and his tongue thrust deep into her mouth, searching and tasting his prey.

At the bed, Barclay knelt, holding the warm and round flesh of the sexy girl in his grasp, and placed her on the bed like food on a plate. Savannah rolled onto her stomach and began to push up to get control. But it was not hers to have control. The vampire was on her with the full force of his want. Barclay felt a surge of strength in his body that was superhuman. He ripped the shirt from his frame and it fell in tatters to the bed. Then grabbing the top of

Savannah's blouse, he shredded it from her body to get to her flesh.

Savannah let out a gasp and a tiny moan as those powerful hands ripped the bra from her frame and pulled her skirt up to her ass in one movement. Her tiny panties were shredded with that same urgent lust of the vampire. "Oh God, oh God, oh God," she whimpered, overwhelmed with the fury of her master and of her own desire to give her body to him and her blood.

The low rumble from the throat of her professor was nothing like a human would make. He fell on her, kissing and biting her ears. She arched back, pushing her butt to him and feeling the hardness of his erection open her butt cheeks and slide around that sensitive flesh. Barclay sucked and kissed along her throat and down to her shoulders, looking down at her ample tits, which were ready to be tasted too. He slid his arms around her middle, mounting the young girl and taking a tit in each hand, squeezing it, and pinching the nipples. That pain only drove Savannah wilder and she orgasmed again.

Her spasms pushed her cunt back to the eager hard cock of the hungry vampire, and it plunged inside her to full depth in one thrust. At the same time, Barclay's mouth found the soft flesh at the edge of Savannah's shoulder just before the arm socket. Those fangs that were so new to Barclay seemed to know what to do. They sank into the flesh of the young girl until blood began to flow over them into his eager mouth.

Savannah felt the pain of the bite and then the blood that was her life flowing into the vampire mouth as he drank from her. Along with that sensation, her vampire lover was squeezing her breasts rhythmically one after the other in tempo with the sucking action so it almost felt like she was feeding him and giving him her life. Then another dramatic sensation hit hard. That stiff cock that had stretched her cunt as though he was taking her cherry began to fuck into her hard and urgently.

In every way, Barclay was making his student's body his food. He fucked her like a wild animal while her blood flowed into him, mauling her generous tits with his fingers. As he felt his orgasm coming, he thrust one hand into her pussy from the front and rubbed her clit hard back and forth and back and forth. The effect was explosive as the biggest orgasm of her life hit her, causing her to double over cumming. She spasmed like she was dying and then fell forward just as the vampire cum began to spew into her deepest womanhood. The poor girl passed out from ecstasy as the wild animal on her pushed up and let his cum flow inside her just as her blood dripped from his lips onto her naked white skin.

Living With Nosferatu

Barclay was glad that Julia was out of town for a month as he sorted out living his life as a college professor by day and vampire by night. Each night, he needed the blood and sex of a young girl. The college was perfect because as he taught his classes in literature, the gorgeous coeds sensed the powerful draw to him. He dined on them in his office or at their dorm or sororities without reservation.

He returned to Savannah's room often and she became a willing slave to his lusts. She brought to him Susanna and Kimberly, and he ravished them on Savannah's bed, ripping their clothing and driving his eager cock into them as he drank from them. He took the blood from different places on each girl. When he made Kimberly his food, he drank her blood from the nip of her left breast. To the innocent girl, it felt so much like the flow coming from her tit was nursing the vampire. And in a way, it was.

As John Duncan had told him, the girls he had drunk from developed an addiction to giving themselves to him again. So Barclay quickly got used to a harem of gorgeous college girls in his office or girls waiting for him in class or in his car to spread their legs to take his cock inside them and then open their veins for him to drink.

"Barclay, I am reading that there may be an infestation of vampires at your school," Julia said over the phone one night. She said this as a skinny blond girl named Alyssa lay naked at his feet, recovering from an orgasm that seemed like it would never end as the vampire fucked her. "That's silly, isn't it?" his worried future wife said to her man.

"It may not be that silly," Barclay said softly, toying with the rim of Alyssa's stretched pussy hole as his cum flowed out of it.

"You aren't in any danger, are you?" she said lovingly.

"No, no, darling," he said softly with a hint of that vampire growl in his voice. That was when the beautiful future bride decided to come home.

On the night she got home, Barclay returned to his house late after fucking two sweet coeds and drinking from them. The smell of their blood was still on his breath.

As soon as he entered the home, she knew something was wrong. What surprised Barclay is that he felt his lust come up from his vampire side even for his beautiful bride. Then he remembered that he needed girls between 18 and 25. Julia had just turned 24.

Julia turned to greet her sweetheart and she jumped in fear at the look in his eyes. His ordinarily soft blue eyes were glowing red. "Bradley, I am worried about the vampire rumor. They say he is making the girls of your college sex slaves," she said, stepping back as he advanced toward her with lust in his eyes.

"It's true; they are slaves to being sucked and drank from," the ordinarily mild mannered college teacher said menacingly. Julia became terrified and confused when she realized it. She just let it out.

"You are the vampire, Barclay?" she gasped. But at the same time, her body was on fire with want to be taken violently by her gentle future husband.

"Yes, the girls are all mine. They are my food. They are my harem," he said, and that is when she saw the faces of dozens of beautiful girls looking into the window.

"Oh God, Barclay," Julia gasped, trying to scream. "Please don't...," she cried out, and that is when his teeth sank into her neck and he began to drink. "Stop!" she whimpered, feeling her orgasm hit with a power of 1000 orgasms. She fell back and gave in to the vampire's lust, opening her legs to feel him violate her cunt and offering him her tits, her pussy, her ass, and all of her blood if he wanted that from her. She would forever become part of the growing army of sexy girls who would be eager to give the accidental vampire all the blood he could ever want and all the pussy he could ever want to fuck as well.

7 THE TENNIS COACH

Gabriella was the most gifted tennis player Kimberly had ever seen. It was as if she were born with a tennis racket in her hand. Kimberly had been coaching tennis at Harrisville University for 12 years. Over that time, she learned to be able to spot talent on the first day the freshmen girls tried out. The results in the form of trophies for the university trophy cabinet said it all, of which Kimberly had put the largest amount of trophies in that cabinet of any other of the many intercollegiate sports in which the college participated.

Alex enjoyed working on campus as a student advisor and library collections expert. It was a desk job so he did not have as much student contact as his wife Kimberly did coaching tennis. But they met when they attended this school two decades earlier, so working on the same campus made them feel like kids again.

It was the first week of training for the tennis team, and Alex dropped by the tennis center to have lunch with Kimberly. He liked to get there early to watch the girls practice. The simple truth was that he loved watching the girls play tennis because their outfits were short and they were nothing if not sexy. But what he told Kimberly is he liked to be able to put faces with names when she told them of their progress at home each evening.

It was easy for Alex to pick out Gabriella from the other girls who were practicing. It was like watching a tennis pro at work and the girl was just barely 18. She simply dominated every match she was in. Her movements were poetry. Another thing kept Alex's attention on the tall slender athlete. She was stunningly beautiful. At one point, he watched as Kimberly helped Gabriella with her swing. As his lovely wife slipped her arms around the middle of that angel to help her with her grasp on the racket, Alex got an erection just from watching that simple and innocent contact.

When the practice was over, Kimberly ran to greet her husband. They exchanged a light kiss and hug and then she said, "Let me introduce you to Gabriella." She called her prodigy over and introduced her to "the love of her life." That was when that sweet and perfectly shaped face smiled and Alex made eye contact. He felt like his heart was going to leap out at that moment as he realized that in the space of a few moments, he had developed a serious crush on that young student.

Office Hours

Experienced teachers and others who work with the student body know that crushes were common. The campus was teeming with thousands of gorgeous young men and women. While their professional profile would never confess it, the staff who deal with those students at all capacities often get little crushes on certain young scholars attending the college for that year. It was spoken of rarely in public, however; Kimberly and Alex talked about it with each other. As long as it was harmless and nothing came of it, there was no danger to their careers or in upsetting a kid by coming on to her or him.

Alex returned to his office after having lunch with his wife to catch up on reports and paperwork. But the image of that phenomenal and very sexy young tennis player stayed in his mind all afternoon. He thought about her long smooth legs and how soft and brown her skin looked. He thought about her small breasts and what her tiny nipples must look like. He thought about the gentle curve of her pussy in that cute tennis outfit and if any unworthy boy had fucked that angelic cunt yet. This was all wildly inappropriate but the thoughts seem to take over his mind.

After Kimberly finished her teaching sessions, she had a meeting with the Dean over the athletic department. She returned to the locker room after the girls had left and changed her clothes. She had a very nice dress ready for the change that cut about three inches above the knee and showed a little bit of shoulder but nothing out of line. She had often seen the Dean glance her body over, so she knew that he liked her nicely shaped butt and breasts. That didn't hurt to get what she wanted in those meetings even though everything stayed quite professional.

She had some time before the meeting so she decided to pop in and see her husband. Working on the same campus gave them lots of chances to see each other, and they often walked hand in hand to the student union for their favorite coffee drink. It reminded them of when they were young students on that campus so many years before. They both liked that part of their careers in higher education very much.

"Guess who?" Kimberly said with a chipper tone to her voice as she walked into Alex's office. Alex as bent over his paperwork and he lit up seeing his gorgeous wife. "Hope you aren't too buried," she said warmly.

"Never too busy to see the love of my life to borrow a phrase," he teased her and she giggled at the reference to his introduction to Gabriella.

"So did you figure out which one Gabriella was as you watched the girls practice?" Kimberly asked. She crossed to the desk and let her butt rest back on the front of the desk, so she was facing her handsome man. Then she leaned down and gave him a little “hello” kiss.

“Hard not to,” Alex answered. “Her talent is amazing. She is going to get you another trophy,” he said, showing his excitement for his wife at having such a talent on her team. Kimberly just giggled because she thought that Gabriella was going to lead her to some big wins this year too. “Not only that,” Alex continued, “I don’t think you have ever had a girl more gorgeous on your team,” he said in a slightly lowered tone.

Kimberly gazed at her husband but not with anger. She reflected on the shape and the beauty of her star tennis player, and she could not disagree with him at all. “You are not the only one who has noticed that,” she said mysteriously.

“She is almost as sexy as her coach,” Alex said slipping his hand between the sexy legs of his wife. She had such a great tan and her legs were so perfectly shaped from being an athlete that she never wore pantyhose.

Instantly Kimberly could tell what her husband wanted. His hand moved between her legs up her thigh stroking and feeling the soft skin of her leg. Being felt up on the top floor of a school administration building was sexy enough, but sitting with her butt pressed against his desk looking at him only made it more exciting.

“Alex, someone could come in,” She gasped as her breathing picked up and her heart rate increased. But when she looked down at his pants, she could tell her husband had a huge erection for her. His 9-

inch penis really made a bulge.

"They will just have to wait their turn."

They could hear people talking in the hallways, and the shades were open to the fourth floor office so down below students were streaming back and forth on their way to classes.

Kimberly leaned back on her hands gasping as her husband began to just take her right in the office. She had not seen him so horny in a while, but she did not connect it with him meeting Gabriella. Alex thrust his tongue in his wife's mouth as his fingers eagerly worked her skirt up her sexy brown thighs. "Oh god yes!" she gasped as she turned her face to the window and saw students she knew down below. At the same time, she felt Alex push his hand inside her panties and begin to stroke up and down her wet pussy slit.

"Fuck me, Alex!"

She gasped, hardly believing this was happening in the middle of the workday on a busy campus. She reached in and unzipped his pants and moved her hand inside to work his underwear down and get a grip on that big sexy cock she loved so much. Looking down at his huge hard cock standing out from his suit pants drove the tennis coach wild with lust.

"Let me take off my panties, Alex."

But Alex had no time for that. He was urgent to get his cock inside his hot wife's wet pussy. He pushed Kimberly back, so she rested more on her hands and planted a massive kiss on her lips sucking her mouth hungrily. At the same time, his skilled fingers pulled the fabric of her soaked panties aside and guided the head of his aching cock to her eager opening.

He plunged inside her so fast and hard that she moaned into his mouth. He trapped her moans of ecstasy in his mouth to keep from alerting people who were actually working and not fucking in their offices. But Alex was fucking the woman he loved the most. He pounded in and out of her hot wet cunt harder and deeper. Kimberly could not remember when he fucked her so ferociously. She latched her arms around his neck for support and thrust back to take every inch of his big cock into her womb. Working as one body, his climax hit like an earthquake, and he exploded inside his wife filling her with cum.

That Championship Season

As the year went by, the success of the college tennis team was just as amazing as they had hoped. The cornerstone of that success was the phenomenal talent of Gabriella. She inspired the team to victory after victory. As is true of most colleges, the sports that usually got all the attention were football and basketball. But this was the year that those sports took a backseat to the inspired playing and leadership of the shy Gabriella. Her skills on the tennis court were the buzz of the tennis world, and there was talk of an amazing championship career once she finished her college years. But she had that big match at the end of the year that would deliver the trophy that everybody wanted.

Only a few days were left before the tennis tournament that would decide which school would own that trophy and which tennis player be declared the best in all of women's tennis. The championship was on the coast so Kimberly had to spend a few days out there making arrangements for the team and meeting with the authorities and the other college coaches about how the tournament would be run.

It was a very cold and wet night, and Alex was at home alone and feeling a little blue. He always missed his wife when she took these trips. He had duties at the school so he could not go with her. It was raining a very cold and drizzly rain out, and the weatherman was saying it would change over to snow before Saturday morning. He built a fire and served himself a drink to try to get cozy enough to go to bed.

It was well after 11 p.m. when the doorbell rang. Alex jumped up fearing that something was wrong and worrying that someone in the family was sick or hurt. When he opened the door, he could not have been more shocked. Standing there in a short rain parka was the school's star tennis player, Gabriella. Not only was she soaked to the skin from the very cold rain, she was weeping.

"Gabriella, what's wrong sweetie?" Alex gasped.

"Mr. Martin, I'm so sorry. I didn't know where to turn. Is coach here?"

"Come in quickly, Gabriella. You are soaked to the skin," Alex said with genuine concern. The young girl got in out of the rain and stood in the entrance hall dripping cold water on the tile. "My wife is on the coast doing preparations for your big tournament, Gabriella. She isn't here."

At that, Gabriella burst into a torrent of tears. Alex could not think of anything to do but hug her and let her drip all over his clothing. "I am so sorry, Mr. Martin."

"Call me, Alex," He whispered.

"I feel so sad and alone and coach has been such a good friend. My sister back home is very sick and my boyfriend was expelled from school for violating the drug regulations to play college football." She wept and her thin tall body just shook in Alex's arms.

"That's ok, sweetie. Just try to calm down. You are safe here. But I am worried about you in those soaked clothes. Let me get you some of Kimberly's things to change into so you don't catch your death of cold."

Gabriella was genuinely touched that Coach Kimberly's husband was so sweet and caring. She felt safe with him. Alex showed her to the bathroom where she could take a hot shower to warm up. Alex ran to the bedroom and grabbed the first thing he could find that would be warm and cozy for the girl to change into. He handed them through the door and she thanked him in a soft but happier voice.

When she walked out both Alex and Gabriella burst out laughing at the silly outfit he had given her. She was wearing what could only be badly mismatched pajamas. The bottoms were bright yellow with bunnies on them and the tops were garish orange with yellow flowers. She also wore some mismatched but cozy socks and a pair of slippers that looked like bears. Gabriella learned a lot that night but one of the things was that her hardworking coach had a little girl side that was silly and very low on taste.

The laughter was healing. Gabriella giggled so hard that she fell forward in those awkward slippers and Alex caught her. It was when his hands passed over her body to grab her arms that he realized she did not have a bra on. His hand brushed her small soft breasts, and for the first time that night, he felt aroused by his guest.

Gabriella hugged Alex and then she sobbed a bit as she laughed. “What’s wrong,” he whispered kissing her lightly on the cheek.

“I am just so glad you were here for me.” Alex brought the young girl to the living room where there was a warm fire going. It had begun to snow outside so he did not want her going out there and she did not want to go. Just then, her cell phone rang from where she had placed it—in the pocket of the pajamas.

She took the call and when she got off, she said with relief that her sister was going to be ok.

“See everything will be fine,” Alex said handing the athlete a glass of wine. “Your sister is fine. You are safe here with me," He continued, "And don't you worry at all about a boyfriend," Alex whispered, his face close to hers. "As beautiful as you are, any boy with a beating heart will want you."

He felt her kiss before he heard the soft "oh" from her lips. The moment was too powerful. The wine, the tears, the fire, the snow, the hugs, the feeling of safety, and the emotions all overcame young Gabriella, and she let her lips touch the husband of her tennis coach. Neither Alex nor Gabriella thought about how wrong it was because that kiss took them over. It started soft and loving and became deep and passionate in moments. Alex slid tongue into the warm lips of the freshman girl, and her mouth opened for him to explore her deeper.

Alex's erection quickly sprang to life and pressed through the light fabric of his shorts against Gabriella's thigh. Gabriella bent her head back and Alex took his time kissing up and down that long, sexy, and slender neck. "You are not like the boys in school," she said, softly stroking the hair of the older man as he sucked her neck. "They just want to fuck me," she moaned in passion.

Alex looked deep into the eyes of the beautiful tennis star. He kissed her gently and whispered, "Don't go out in that storm. I want you to stay here tonight. I want to take care of you." When he said that, tears began to stream down her angelic face and she put a long, soft, and wet kiss on his lips.

"That is why I want you to fuck me," she whispered as she kissed his ear and neck.

Alex almost shot his load when she said that to him. Instead, he stood up and lifted her in his arms to take her to the bed where he and his wife slept together. Gabriella and Alex kissed deeply like newlyweds as he took her to his bed. As he looked at this almost perfect young girl in his bed, Alex thought for a moment that he should not fuck her. But when he held her delicate hand out to him and said softly, "I want to please you," there was no turning back.

Pulling off his shirt, he fell into bed with the gorgeous and sexy Gabriella. She was so full of emotion that she gave herself fully to him. Those funny pajamas were loose on her so as he kissed her; he easily slid his hand under her top to begin to caress her small breasts. The nipples were tiny but hard from arousal. Gently he laid her head on the soft pillow and pulled her top off. As he made love to her nipples, he slid the pajama bottoms down those long sexy legs.

The feel of the naked 18-year-old girl in his bed drove Alex to heights of passion. They kissed deeply like they needed it to survive. He rolled her onto her back and she eagerly opened her slender legs to give him access to her pussy. Getting out of his shorts, he let her gaze at his very long and hard cock before he laid between her legs to mate with her.

"Oh, God, Mr. Martin, it's stretching me!" the girl moaned as Alex's stiff penis opened her pussy hole and filled it up. Soon he was thrusting into her faster and faster, fucking her with a fury that he didn't know he was capable of. “Take me, Mr. Martin!” she moaned “Fuck me!” as she fucked up to let every inch of that long cock make her insides his own. Just as she hit her peak and cried out loudly with her orgasm, he came too filling her with cum.

The Big Match

Gabriella stayed the weekend with Alex, and they made love in that bed countless times. She never felt so happy and she even let the thought in her mind that she may be in love with him. Aside from making her cum like no high school or college boy ever did, he cooked meals for her, they watched movies, and they developed a deep and lasting love and friendship.

Gabriella was scheduled to fly to San Diego for the competition on Monday morning. Alex took her by her apartment to get her things together and then drove her to the airport. Their kiss goodbye in the parking garage resulted in her climbing on top of him and pulling her skirt up so he could fuck her one more time before leaving for the week.

The preparations for the matches were intense. Gabriella had to put her wild love affair with the tennis coach’s husband aside so she could focus on winning. And win she did. She eliminated one competitor after the other rolling through the tournament and attracting a lot of attention. Gabriella was pleased that her strong friendship with Coach Kimberly was still intact. Of course Kimberly did not know of the affair, and

Gabriella stilled cared about her very much and needed her coaching. This was especially true after she won the semifinal match. After the win, Gabriella went back to the gym area of the facility at the host college for a cool down time. She was jogging on the track when she fell.

The phone in the suite that Kimberly had rented for the week rang and the panicked sound of Gabriela's voice upset the coach a great deal. After calming the emotional teenager down, Kimberly learned of the fall and that Gabriella had soreness in her hip and thigh as a result of the accident. "Now calm down Gabriella and come over to my suite. Go slow so you do not injure it further. We can get you ready for the match tomorrow."

Kimberly stayed calm but she was worried. This last match was for the trophy and the championship. But Kimberly had gotten great tennis players through issues like this before and gone on to the win. That is why she has so many trophies back at home.

Gabriella got to the room rather late. As soon as Kimberly explained that a strained muscle can be wrapped so she could still win, the girl calmed down. Kimberly had a massage table set up for situations like this that she had ordered with the room. "Gabriella, take off your pants so I can examine the hurt muscle." She instructed the girl.

As the tennis star peeled her outer workout pants away, she only had her regular cotton panties on and her light exercise shirt. She got up on the massage table on her belly and made herself comfortable with the pillow. Kimberly put on some jazz music to help calm the girl as the injury had unnerved her considerably.

Kimberly used soft and soothing tones telling Gabriella that everything was going to be fine and praising her for the success she has had. At times, it seemed like the young athlete almost purred from this treatment. Kimberly was an expert at giving tender loving care to the fragile emotions of a championship athlete.

Her fingers began to gently massage the flesh of the beautiful girl. As she felt the stimulation of flesh on flesh, she wished her sexy husband Alex was here to fuck her when this was done. She did not know that laying there being touched, Gabriella also wished she could be under Alex feeling his big hard cock inside her.

The muscle group that was sore was at the top of the thigh just below the hip. Kimberly found that spot and gently but skillfully worked it. The thigh was wider there and the flesh warm and brown. As Kimberly felt that private skin of the young girl, she noticed Gabriella's thin panties shift as her tight and small butt cheeks shifted to the massage.

Kimberly eyes were frozen on the crotch of those panties. Each time the leg moved, that crotch fabric moved and Kimberly got a look at her beautiful pussy. Kimberly was hypnotized by that sight. She had never had sex with a girl but she suddenly felt her heart speeding up and that familiar tingle in her nipples and cunt. In spite of herself, Kimberly was getting excited.

"Oh yes don't stop!" Gabriella moaned and that moan had a sensual sound to it. That is when Kimberly felt brave and she pushed the fabric of the panties aside. As her left hand gave relief to the muscle of that sexy thigh, the fingers of the right hand touched the lip of Gabriella's sex. She stroked that pouty flesh and pulled it back as her thumb pushed the panty further apart.

Kimberly was so drawn to the pussy of her star tennis player that she barely noticed Gabriella spreading her thighs to give her coach a better view. Not before long that Kimberly had pulled the entire crotch of the panty aside, and her fingers had spread that pink slit wide open. She gazed with awe and desire at the sweet fleshy vagina opening never knowing her husband had been fucking that hole for 48 hours.

Kimberly forgot all about the injured thigh as she ran her fingers up and down the hidden folds of that sweet young cunt. When she found Gabriella's clitoris, any pretending was over. Gabriella moaned and wiggled in pleasure as her coach stroked her clit and played with the slit of her sex. When Gabriella pushed the fabric of her panties down over her butt, Kimberly silently obeyed and slid the panties off and put them on the couch.

When she returned, Gabriella had turned

over and was looking up at the coach that she loved. Her legs were wide open for Kimberly to explore. “I love you, Coach Kimberly,” Gabriella said and that only added more confusion to a mind and was out of control trying to keep up. Kimberly leaned over to the beautiful face of her sweet star athlete and kissed her deeply. When that kiss finally paused, Gabriella whispered, “Make love to me.”

The massage table was no longer able to keep up with the two girls who were discovering their lesbian love. The suite was empty so Gabriella got up and stripped away her top walking to the luxurious bedroom. Shyly, the wife, coach, and college teacher stripped nude and climbed into bed with the slender 18-year-old beauty. The kisses were deep and soulful. Gabriella could not get enough of Kimberly's larger breasts, and as they cuddled under the covers, Gabriella kissed and sucked them lovingly.

Finally, Kimberly rolled over onto Gabriella and laid between her legs. She held the side of her head and kissed her deeply and put one thigh over the young girl's thigh so their pussies pressed into each other. Working carefully, each girl fit the slit of her pussy to the other and they began to grind. Their passions took over and they thrust into each other kissing and moaning. It was hard to tell if Kimberly was fucking Gabriella or the other way around. But that stimulation drove the excited tennis coach over the top and she orgasmed in wild spasms. Gabriella thrust up to the pussy of her coach and came hard holding Kimberly to her and kissing her deeply.

They made love all night. The next day Gabriella played like she was born again. She was a champion because of the love of her coach. Kimberly arranged to stay one more day in San Diego, and she made it a special day of love and discovering their ability to make each other come in dozens of ways. That night before they fell asleep in each other's arms, covered in each other's juices, Kimberly whispered, "I want my sweet Alex to enjoy you. I want him to fuck you." And she kissed Gabriella. All Gabriella could say to her lover and coach was, "yes my love."

8 TAKEN BY A GHOST

Stephanie

"When will Anna be here?" Aaron asked his wife Stephanie. Their niece Anna was going to spend a year with them and work on her college dissertation at the University of California. The campus at Berkley wasn't close so she would have to drive there on days she needed to gather research. However, her aunt and uncle had set up a nice office for her and had given her one of the better rooms in the inn to live in for free all year.

"She will be here this evening," Stephanie answered.

Aaron and Stephanie bought the old inn when it was run-down. The family that sold it needed the money, but it had been in their family for centuries. The inn sat atop a cliff that looked out over the ocean. Below were the remains of a once busy dock where tall ships came in for sailors to enjoy the hospitality of the inn. That was long ago. But even to this day, the rumours of hauntings continue to lend a lot of lore to the inn that Aaron and Stephanie now ran. In many ways, it seemed to help business more than to hurt it. Of course the amazing view of the sea didn't hurt any either. The outcome was that the Sea Mist Inn was a big success.

Aaron stood behind his wife as she gazed out of the third floor window of their bedroom suite. They both loved the inn with its gothic architecture, but at times, the history of the place seemed to want to take them over. He gazed out of that big window with the stained glass accents and the sea looked angry out there. He hated to see her look so distracted and down this early in the morning.

"I had that dream again."

She had a slow and solemn tone to her voice. Aaron gently slipped his arms around her middle as she gazed out on the angry sea and held her for comfort.

"It was another time. I was not with you in this warm and safe inn. I was on a ship and the sea was tossing us about like toys. You were not there, my darling husband. The men on the ship were hardened men of the sea. Even they were getting sick from the waves. Then I saw him."

Stephanie was no longer in her husband's gentle arms in her mind. She had entered that dream and was living it as she spoke it.

"He was a head taller than the other

rough men. He took me and dragged me to a stateroom on the rough ship. He threw me on the bed. The ship tossed and I was thrown off the bed, but he did not budge. With one hand he pulled me to the bed and pushed up my skirt to fuck me."

Aaron felt his wife pushing back against his body and felt her arms clawing at his pants. Her eyes were closed as she swooned into the vision of being made the sex slave of a rough sailor who died on a ship off the coasts that were just below the rocky cliffs of the inn. Aaron knew that this was no dream. This was an encounter with the beyond.

"Yes Captain Stolz, fuck your slave girl."

As his wife moaned, Aaron felt his own cock grow rock-hard and he pulled up her simple cotton dress and pushed it over her hips. Forcefully he pushed her forward so she had to lean on the windowsill with her head out in brisk winds that swept along the coast of California that time of year.

He grabbed her panties and pushed them down with as much force as he could. He knew that while he was going to fuck his own wife, in her mind she was giving herself to her master, the ghost of Captain Stolz. Captain Stolz died along with his crew when his ship, the Sea Mist, sank in a storm just miles off shore of where their inn faced out to sea. All perished in that shipwreck and the ghosts of the Sea Mist inhabited their inn; that is why the inn carried on the name of that doomed ship.

Aaron thrust his fingers into the hot cunt between his wife's sexy legs. Her vagina was oozing wet and hot with desire. Quickly he yanked open his pants and released his rock-hard cock to fuck her both for his own lust and to release her from her vision. He leaned and kissed her hard on the neck, sucking it forcefully. She opened her legs wide to let her master fuck her deep from behind. In one thrust, Aaron rammed his cock deep into his wife and began to fuck her against the bedroom window.

"The boat is breaking up!"

Stephanie gasped as she gave her wet pussy to the ghost captain. "Fuck me as we die!" she cried out with her head hanging out of the window so the guests and strangers heard those eerie moans down the wind.

"Drive it deep into me again and again!" she screamed and Aaron fucked her in exact synchronization to the movements of the ghost captain as he fucked his wife. Suddenly Stephanie moaned loudly and orgasmed. At the same time, she virtually screamed "We are lost!" and she swooned just as her husband shot his load deep in his pussy hole.

Sophia

Aaron and Stephanie busied themselves with guests and the affairs of running a busy inn, and that distracted them from the disturbing images that had haunted them. The gloomy fog hung around all day like it was not done with the Sea Mist Inn. Aaron went from room to room to make sure that the rooms where guests had checked out or that were to be rented were in good condition. It was on the second floor that he noticed the fog coming in the hallway windows as he entered one of the rooms.

When Aaron came out, he was startled that the fog was so thick around that window that he could not see the wall. It even dimmed the lights in the hallway. As he was locking the door, he thought he heard a soft whisper of a name. Then he looked closer in the middle of the mist where he saw a figure. It was slender with long hair. Aaron could barely make out the shape of breasts and wider hips so he felt certain it was the shape of a young woman in the middle of the fog. Then she spoke that name again and vanished. That name was *Jared.*

Stephanie left to pick up Anna at 4 p.m. It was a long trip to the San Francisco Airport since the inn was located so far north of the city. Aaron had some time to poke around the journals that they found in the inn that revealed more about the wreck of the Sea Mist in 1872, which still affects the inn to this day. The journals were kept in Room 448, which was one floor above their bedroom. They rarely rented it out because it seemed the incidents of hauntings were more frequent and more disturbing in that room.

It was getting dark in the room and Aaron sat on the bed facing the closet where the old journals were found. The window to his left brought in the mist of the sea and the continuous sound of the sea below. Behind him, the door was open because that made him feel less isolated in the spooky room. His rational side told him that the ghosts of the Sea Mist were just stories that brought in customers. But the feelings coming out of the many paintings around the inn of Captain Stolz and others and the sighting and his and his wife's encounters with the dead but not gone told him otherwise.

Suddenly the air in the room felt colder and Aaron got chills. He had a strong feeling he was not alone. He turned and confirmed it when he saw a young woman standing in the doorway. He had seen her mixing in at the wine and cheese party the inn holds each evening. She had a faraway and haunting look to her. However, she was pretty in a sweet and troubled way. Her light brown hair was wispy around her face and neck. She was petite and slender with a slight bust line, and her hips were round but not bulging at all.

"This is my room," the girl said in a soft voice looking right at him.

"No sweetie, this room is not rented out. I am the owner of the inn and I am just looking at some things we have in here," Aaron said. But as he said that, he suddenly realized that from the shape, this was the girl standing in the fog when he was in the hallway earlier that day. He suddenly felt uneasy about this encounter.

"This has always been my room," the girl said, looking off toward the window. "It was my room for my lover to be with me before he sailed away on the Sea Mist. They said that my Jared perished when the Sea Mist vanished, but I waited for him. For years...centuries, I waited for him," she said, crossing to the window and gazing out to the sea.

Aaron stood and slowly approached the ghostly girl. "Sophia?" he said softly, remembering the name of the girl from the ghost stories of the inn and from the books.

He was confused because he had seen her mixing with the guests, eating, drinking, touching people. If she was Sophia, she has been dead for over a century. Sophia was married to Captain Stolz. The captain was 20 years older than her, and he did abduct women and molest them on board his ship as Aaron's wife had sensed in their experience that morning. Sophia fell in love with one of the sailors on board of the Sea Mist. They had torrid love affair in Room 448, which was Sophia's home while she was staying there with her aunt and uncle after the death of her parents.

Sophia was driven mad with grief when the Sea Mist sank and the news made it back to the mainland. She refused to believe that her beloved Jared drowned. She stayed on watch on the roof of the inn day and night, looking out to the sea for him, never eating or sleeping. Finally, in her weakened state up there on the roof, she thought she saw Jared come and visit her there. In the explosion of love that she experienced, she rushed to his arms only to plunge over the edge to the rocks below.

When Sophia heard her name said softly, she turned suddenly facing Aaron. Their eyes locked and Aaron was captivated by the young girl. She looked in his eyes like she knew him.

"Jared?" she said with soft excitement, reaching up to his face and stroking his cheek with her soft fingers. Aaron was shocked to feel how warm and exciting the skin of the ghostly girl was on his face. As her lips met his, he heard the door of the suite close behind them. He understood in his sixth sense that she had done that, but the frightening implications of making love to an insane young woman who was also a ghostly haunting did not cut through to his mind. He felt like the 24-year-old boy she thought he was. "Jared, do you still love me?" she whispered in his ear as she kissed it.

"Yes, Sophia," Aaron said and they kissed deeply. When her tiny tongue slid into his mouth, he sucked that ancient tongue that felt in eerie way like the warm human tongue of a 20-year-old girl. As a ghost, she had never aged.

"Oh Jared," she gasped as he lowered her to the bed. "It has been 100 years that I have waited for you to fuck me. Satisfy me again," she moaned. She lay back on the bed and Aaron eagerly lifted her simple worker's dress, revealing the tanned and slender thighs of the deceased young woman. When Aaron felt his penis begin to get stiff, he was freaked out and more excited than he had ever been before at the same time.

Aaron ran his hands up the soft young legs of the ancient Sophia and her sighs reflected not having this pleasure for a century. Then Aaron began to kiss those sweet legs. He could not explain how it could be, but the flesh was warm and sweet to the taste. He felt his cock go completely erect in his pants and he unzipped to give it relief.

"Oh my lover, fuck me," Sophia whispered in heaven at the feel of Aaron's kisses on her thighs. Aaron could think of nothing else but fucking this beautiful sweet ghost girl. He slid her simple panties down, revealing the soft fur of her pussy. Her delicate cunt lips were pouting out, aroused by his attention. Quickly he stood and pushed down his pants to take her right there on the same bed she fucked Jared on over a hundred years before.

Aaron leaned over, kissed the lovely maiden from the past, and opened her sweet wet slit with his fingers. He fit the head of his cock into her tight hole and felt the resistance of a vagina that had not been fucked for over a hundred years. Suddenly the spirit of the rough seaman Jared seemed to have taken over. Aaron pushed up on the arms of the adorable Sophia and, in one rough thrust, buried his cock inside her.

Suddenly the room was swirling and more was going on than Aaron could figure out. He felt the tight cunt of the young ghost girl take his hard cock completely inside herself. His ears were split by the gasp of excitement and pain Sophia let out at feeling her Jared fill her pussy hole again. Along with that, a wind rushed into the room and carried the joined bodies of the lovers away. Aaron pulled Sophia to him and fucked her, not knowing where they were. They were lost in passion as she thrust back, moaning out "Oh yes" to him.

Before he could catch his wits, he pushed up and rammed his hard cock to the balls inside of the 20-year-old ghost. His testicles were exploding with cum and it erupted inside the little thing. Sophia felt living cum fill her cold insides for the first time and she arched up and orgasmed so powerfully that it threw Aaron completely free of her.

Aaron saw the sky over him and looked up at the cliffs. They were on the beach where they both had the biggest orgasm either had ever experienced in any lifetime. Aaron landed in the shallow surf of the beach. He struggled to his feet to see the beautiful Sophia on the beach standing with her garments dishevelled from the fresh fucking she had enjoyed. Their eyes met and he fought the water to get back to her. But just as quickly she became his lover, she was gone with only a swirl of fog left behind.

Anna

Stephanie picked up Anna at the San Francisco Airport and they enjoyed a good meal in the city. The drive back to the Sea Mist Inn was a long one. But it was good to catch up on family gossip and have some normal girl time before Anna had to set up her office in the inn and buckle down on her dissertation.

Anna was fascinated with the stories of the ghosts at the Sea Mist. The stories were so well known that there had been features made about them on those shows that pretend to look for ghosts. The TV crews had come to the inn and all it took was a good stiff breeze up the cliffs to make them think they had evidence. This all, of course, was great for business.

Stephanie had looked at the books in Room 448 so she knew the facts of what happened. The ill-fated merchant ship went to the bottom of the Pacific, carrying Jared, the rough Captain Stolz, and the rest of the crew to a watery grave. She also knew about the tragic story of Sophia and the many sightings of the lovesick girl still haunting the inn. Stephanie laughed it all off to superstition and good marketing because she did not want to frighten the sweet child with the reality of what she had experienced at the hands of the horny old ghost captain of the Sea Mist.

"Is Uncle Aaron well?" Anna asked politely. She did not know her uncle very well. In fact, Aaron entered the family when Anna was almost nine, although Stephanie and Aaron had been renovating the Sea Mist Inn for many years before they became romantic partners and then a married couple. Anna was looking forward to getting to know her uncle a little better.

Some time had passed since the encounter with Sophia for Aaron to recover before his wife and niece showed up. He had to climb the steep path up from the beach where their wild fuck had landed him. His clothing was wet and torn from the supernatural fall to the beach. How that did not kill him, he had no idea. It was no good asking logical questions when he knew he was fucking a cute 20-year-old ghost as it was happening.

By the time the girls drove up from their long road trip, Aaron was sitting in the community room with a couple of guests enjoying a brandy while watching the fire burn. When the door opened and Stephanie sang out "It's us!" Aaron rushed out to greet the girls. But when he walked into the entryway, he jumped back and gasped. "Sweetie, is everything okay?" his wife said with concern at the way the color had drained from his face.

"No, no, I am fine."

But he could hardly stop looking at Anna. She was in every possible way an identical image of the long dead Sophia whose face and body Aaron would never forget after this night.

The three family members visited for quite a while before Aaron helped his niece to her room. She too had a sea view on the fourth floor. Her room was just three doors down from Room 448. Aaron felt some concern about it, but that was the room they had prepared for family visitors long before the eerie events and visitations began. But they would still keep Room 448 well secured so that Anna might be spared from the visitations.

Anna retired to her room and looked over the window. It was pitch black but there was a full moon so she could see the breakers on the sea, which was a big part of why she wanted to be at the Sea Mist to do her work. Having grown up in the Midwest, she was excited at the thought of spending a year at a strange gothic inn on the coast of California. Throw in a few ghosts and she was all prepared for an adventure.

Anna had the lights down in the room and she had changed into her nightgown. It was a one piece that was quite sheer so she was a bit chilled from the mist coming off from the ocean. But she was in love with the sea already. She was about to retire when she thought she heard something outside. Of course, the beach was far below the steep cliff so it was silly that anyone was out there. However, as she lay in her bed, she heard it again. It was a soft voice, like the wind was speaking. It said only one word.

"Sophia."

Anna was troubled in her sleep. She fought off believing that she heard that voice in the night. She had gone to bed late after listening to the stories of Jared and Captain Stolz and Sophia. No wonder her imagination took it from there. But in the morning, she found footprints in the carpet of her room. They were boot prints that were wet with seaweed lying around too. They were fresh.

The next day was busy with exploring the grounds, the beach, and the cliffs. Anna set up her office on the ground floor of the land side of the inn. It had been an old library so it had the perfect atmosphere for writing and research. The stories of ghosts and the strange occurrences in her room the night before were not far from her mind. She did not say anything to her aunt or uncle. She seemed so sure it was all silly.

After lunch, Anna went up to her room to freshen up and change clothes. She had passed Room 448 several times and wondered why there was a padlock on it. One time she stopped in front of it and she thought she heard footsteps. But when she went up after lunch, the padlock was open and the door was open a bit.

Anna could not resist her curiosity. When she pushed open the door, she saw a regular room. But on the bed were some large dusty books open. She did not know that her aunt and uncle would never leave those books out like that. Anna walked over to the books and found the pictures and other information about the wreck of the Sea Mist and the fates Sophia and Jared. She was so involved in the book that she did not hear the door swing shut. Suddenly she felt a chill. She stood up and slowly backed away from the book until she backed into the dresser that had a mirror over it.

When she spun around, Anna screamed. There in the mirror was a girl who looked exactly like her, but she was not moving as Anna was moving. “Who are you?” she gasped. The girl in the mirror looked puzzled.

"Sophia."

And then the girl in the mirror said, "I am you!"

Anna ran in panic from the room.

Over the next week, even though appearances became more frequent, they were never expected. Anna became anxious at what might appear around each corner. As she was walking in the garden, there was a slender gardener bent over the flowers. When he looked at her, the beautiful face of Jared gazed at her with shining eyes, and he whispered the name, "Sophia." Sitting with her aunt and uncle watching the fire, she turned and saw a figure in the window. That figure looked like her, but it was that ghostly girl.

When Anna saw that, she let out a stifled scream and put her hand over her mouth.

"Are you all right, sweetie?" her aunt asked with concern.

"Yes, I just need to lie down, I think," Anna said and she left the family time to go to her room. As Anna climbed the stairs, she felt the presence of the ghosts near her. She felt she was being guided to her room, but as she walked past Room 448, she entered it without thinking. She felt like she was in a haze and her mind was not her own. She felt like she was guided to the bed, and she lowered onto it, lying facing upward on the soft mattress.

Suddenly Anna felt fingers on her legs. Her skirt was being pushed up. Part of her was terrified but another part felt like this was a step to fulfilling her destiny. When she looked down, the lovely Sophia was gazing up at her lovingly. Sophia knelt between Anna's legs and pushed her skirt over her hips. In a wave, it seemed like Anna's panties just disappeared and Sophia leaned in and parted the folds of her pussy.

Anna was not bisexual but the feel of the ghostly girl stroking her slit and beginning to lick her sensitive clitoris drove Anna wild. She reached down to hold Sophia's head, and her hair was soft and almost like air. Soon Anna was moaning and thrusting her face up to the tongue of the ghost girl. She felt her orgasm might come, but instead, when she looked up, she saw the face of another. It was Jared kneeling on the bed and putting his hand on the back of Anna's head to draw her to him.

"My sweet Sophia."

Anna's mind was racing as she glanced down at the girl between her legs. But instead of a slender and sexy girl licking her cunt, Anna saw that figure transform into a mist. It swirled over her spread-wide thighs, and then slowly it began to spiral like a tornado. The top of the tornado found its way to the opening of Anna's pussy, and in a swift whoosh, Sophia filled Anna up from the inside.

The sudden surge of feelings when that ghost possessed her caused Anna to gasp and push up into the arms of Jared. He kissed her deeply and peeled his sailor's shirt off, showing his very sexy chest. He pulled Anna fully onto the bed and pulled her blouse open, revealing her naked tits to him.

"I have yearned for the fleshy nipples of my Sophia," Jared said as he leaned in and began to suck Anna, moving from one hard nipple to the next.

"Oh my Jared." Anna heard her voice saying, but it was not her saying it. "Fuck your Sophia." The Anna part of her mind was getting smaller and weaker. The thoughts of lust and love for her ancient lover that came from the possessing spirit of Sophia took over. Whoever was in charge, her body was responding to the eager touch and licking the ghostly boy on top of her was doing to her in that bed. "I have life in this body now, Jared." Sophia moaned as Jared pushed his sailor's pants down to release his big hard cock. "Fuck this body and take your own life back from it," she finished.

Jared was eager to make that transformation. Lifting Anna and Sophia's sexy body to his, he held her tight butt cheeks and pulled her wet pussy up to go inside it. She felt his mouth and teeth on her shoulder sucking and biting and then the plunge of that huge cock filling up her tight hole. Sophia felt more alive than ever since the shipwreck as her lover began to fuck his hard cock in and out of her.

"Oh God, yes," she gasped and his thrusts got deeper and harder. The young girl came alive as she thrust back up to take as much of his big cock into her as she could get. Working like one body, the two ancient lovers fucked in sync with his powerful hips ramming that long hard dick into her again and again and again.

"I am going to explode inside of you," Jared moaned into the ear of his lover.

"Explode in me, darling. Make us eternal," she moaned back, biting his ear and wanting to feel his cum inside her.

Down in the sitting room, Aaron and Stephanie heard the loud scream of their niece, Anna, yelling out the biggest orgasm of her life. They dashed up to the stairs, and before they got to her room, they saw the door open to Room 448. They entered but they did not find the body of their beautiful niece there. Instead, it looked like an explosion had happened on the bed. The bedclothes were scattered all over the room with burn marks on them. The window was wide open and the shutters were blown off completely.

"Oh God, Aaron," Stephanie wept. "Do you think she is dead?" Just then, Aaron gasped as he looked out to the sea.

"No, Stephanie, look." As Anna's aunt stepped to the window beside her husband, she saw just offshore, in a heavy sea mist, the ancient ship that had sunk so long ago. Standing on the deck looking at them was the young sailor who had haunted their inn, Jared. A beautiful young woman was standing next to him, arms around his middle and glowing with the happiness of a young bride.

"Oh my God, Aaron, that's Anna."

"No, it isn't, Stephanie. That is Sophia. It always has been Sophia. And it always will be."

9 WHAT ALIENS WANT

Prologue

"What's wrong with us Jack?" Melissa asked in a slightly teasing way looking across the table at her oldest friend in the world. "Are we just too hideous for someone to ever want to stay with us more than a few months?" The two had been discussing their romantic woes. While Melissa was 28 and Jack was 29, they could hardly be considered over the hill. But for both friends, settling down with that perfect romantic partner seemed as far away as some spacecraft that abducted people to their home planet for experiments.

Jack and Melissa liked to try the new restaurants around town. They had been best friends since childhood, and their friendship has helped them through the ups and downs of many romances. Jack always liked that scene from "When Harry Met

Sally" where Harry says it is impossible for a man to be friends with a woman without having sex with her. Their friendship was proof that they could do it year after year.

Jack knew that Melissa was a lovely girl with a very nice figure. But he never felt the temptation to come on to her. Melissa often thought to herself that there was no question that Jack was a good-looking guy. He worked out and that gave him a sculpted body. He looked great on the beach in the summer. She wondered why girls were not crawling all over him. But in her eyes, he was the perfect guy friend, and since they had enjoyed a deep friendship for their whole lives, she would never jinx that with a romance.

They had heard good things about Nostromo, and those who had eaten there said it was a life changing experience. Jack drove to the place as they had their talk about their romantic woes. When they arrived, they walked around a hedge that went up to the restaurant. Suddenly, two girls came running out almost knocking them down.

They were both very pretty, but their hair and clothing were a mess like they had been in an accident. They were both gasping and crying weeps that were mixed with little squeaks of terror. The taller of the young girls ran right into Jack. He pulled her to a stop trying to stabilize her. "Girls it is ok. You are safe. What is going on?" he said with sincere concern.

"Don't go in there," the girl Jack held said

with a wild look in her eyes. “We were abducted by aliens after eating there,” she said weeping.

“They did sex experiments on us,” the second one almost screamed, clawing at Melissa.

“We had to do sex to each other!” the first girl yelled.

“We had to make out, and I had to lick her pussy,” the short one claimed. “Oh god, oh god, oh god,” she continued. “It was so hot!” She went on which did not make sense as out of control frightened as they were. But suddenly, the girls broke free of Jack and Melissa and embraced and kissed each other deeply, tearing each other’s clothing.

“I had to suck her tits,” the blond wildly yelled as she shoved her hand into her friend’s panties finding her pussy.

“I had to finger her cunt,” the other said falling to the ground as her friend fell on her. “And her butt hole!”

Jack and Melissa got away from the wild girls. Their only explanation was that the girls were under the influence of drugs. They got to the steps of the restaurant and tried to gather their wits. They decided not to let it ruin their evening.

The dinner was amazing. Jack had the steak and Melissa enjoyed a pasta dish. She was so in love with it; she made Jack take a bite as they both enjoyed the house made special wine.

Where Are We?

Jack woke up in a place he did not know.

The rooms were all white, and he was lying on a single bed looking up at bright lights. He sat up and his head hurt immediately. He let his mind search back to what happened. He remembered sitting in that restaurant with Melissa having a sip of very good wine. There was no memory after that.

"JACK?"

Melissa's voice came from another room, and she sounded terrified. The small bedroom had one door that went out into a larger room that was also white and sterile looking. Jack rushed out.

Melissa was coming out of the room right next to his.

"Oh Jack!" she wept and she ran to him full of fear. "Where are we?"

"I am not sure Melissa."

The room was far too bright with glaring lights that made up the entire ceiling. In the room, there was a large bed, a few cabinets and some comfortable lounge chairs as well. Suddenly, that glaring light vanished. They were plunged into darkness.

Just as suddenly, the walls turned into a huge display of panels. All along the upper part of the tall room, Jack and Melissa saw dozens of beings staring down at them from behind windows.

"Jack, what are they?"

"Aliens. We have been abducted Melissa."

The figures were otherworldly in every way. They had tiny slender frames with huge heads that had huge sunken eyes. Their faces were like skulls and their mouth were just square outlets with no lips. There were terrifying to look at as they used their bony fingers to point at their victims in their laboratory.

"No Jack, this is crazy."

Jack turned toward her and held her arms.

"Remember what those girls said? It must have been true. Something about that restaurant is a front for aliens abducting people."

He tried to sort it out as he explained it to her. She was babbling in terror so Jack just pulled her to his chest. "Listen Melissa, I am here. We will get through this. We just have to stick together. I won't leave you."

"But what do they want?"

She didn't have to wait long. Like they knew she had asked, the images of the aliens suddenly disappeared, and a large video screen came on. Without a second to figure things out, Jack and Melissa were assaulted with videos of a woman sucking a man's hard cock. Neither of the friends watched pornography, so that image shocked them. But then thinking about those girls, they knew what the aliens wanted.

Just as fast, the video stopped and a spot light hit Jack just illuminating the crotch of his pants. Then an eerie voice came over the loudspeaker talking in some alien language. It was demanding, but there was no way they could understand the words. The voice was high and shrill like you might imagine an insect would sound if it could talk. The light flashed like it was making a point.

Then the voice spoke angrily.

"They want you to take it out."

"NO."

Jack said, and just as fast as he said it, an electric jolt hit the brass wristbands they both were wearing. Jack yelped and fell back on the bed. The light was on his crotch again and that demanding voice.

"Please Jack. Let me do it."

She was not able to stand seeing her sweet friend tortured. Jack was shaken by the jolt, but he let her do it. Melissa walked to the edge of the bed, stood between his open legs and unzipped his pants. Reaching in, she pushed aside his underwear and found his cock. She worked slowly like a nurse. She was shocked how huge Jack's cock was. She pulled it out, and though he did not want it to happen, it started to get hard.

"Melissa, I am so sorry. I don't know what is happening to me."

Just then, Melissa felt a little faint and she sat on the bed.

"Me, too. Something is happening inside me. I am tingling all over. They must have drugged us. My boobs are tingling, and I am getting wet in my privates Jack."

As she spoke, Jack's nine-inch cock got harder and harder in front of her. Jack was embarrassed but turned on in a way he could not understand.

The spotlight hit that hard cock and that voice shouted orders. Then the spot pointed to Melissa in the face, went back to his cock, and then to her face. The video came on showing the porn woman sucking cock.

"Melissa, you know what they are demanding?"

"Yes, they want me to suck your cock Jack."

"No, Melissa lets fight them. I don't want our friendship to change."

Just then another jolt his arm bonds and he fell back on the bed in shock breathing heavily.

"I won't let them hurt you anymore."

With that, she reached over, took that huge hard penis in her hand, and moved her hand up and down it. Soon she was hypnotized by the beautiful cock. As she played with it, the lights became less harsh. Some soft lamps came on in the room and a music system somewhere started playing smooth jazz. The couple learned that this meant their captors were happy with them. Melissa felt less anxious because she was pleasuring a guy she cared about very much.

"Does that feel good Jack?"

"Oh yes Melissa. Yes"

"We will get through this together."

She whispered, and at that, she put her lips to the mushroomed head. She kept the images from the video the aliens had on as a guide. She let her tongue find the skin and licked his cock slowly tasting it. When a bubble of fluid came out, it got on her tongue but she did not react. She lapped it up and decided to love Jack through this even if he did just make pee. Of course, it was pre-cum.

"I am going to suck it now."

"Ok."

He felt her mouth take the head of his horny cock inside. At first, she sucked it like it was a candy or like she was trying to drink out of it. That felt amazing to Jack and he moaned.

"I am so turned on Melissa."

"Me too," she answered and then she copied the video and began sucking his cock and licking the shaft up and down. She took the hard meat deeper in her mouth and moved it in and out of her lips. She felt so excited and adult sucking the hard penis of her best friend.

"Oh God yes."

He moaned holding her head. Soon his fucking reflex kicked in, and he began to thrust his hard prick in and out of her soft lips. He felt her tongue massaging the sensitive skin of his head inside her mouth and he began to fuck her mouth faster and faster.

"Oh God, Melissa, I am going to...."

But it was too late. A huge stream of warm cum shot from his mouth and hit the back of Melissa's mouth. Before it could ooze down her throat, another shot out as Jack came in fast shots in her eager lips. She responded by instinct and swallowed the cum. She let it ooze out of mouth onto her face and neck. It seemed like forever, but finally, he slowed and they just lay there on that bed with aliens watching holding each other and using the sheets to wipe the cum off of each other.

All the Way

After a while, the lights came on. The videos stopped, and it was like they were in an empty building. Jack and Melissa explored their setting and found bathrooms. It was clear that the aliens knew what humans needed. This perverted scientific setup was equipped for them to live there as long as the aliens wanted to keep them and play with them.

When they came out, there was a table set with food and wine on it. Time went by in that place where nothing happened. Food was provided and the lights went off at a specified time that signaled it was night. Melissa and Jack talked about if they were in space, on a faraway planet or on earth in some underground bunker the aliens had built. There was no way of knowing that. Jack explored every room of their living quarters. There were closets with clothing that fit. The aliens were thorough. Jack tried to find any place where there might be an opening for escape. There was none.

At least they had each other. The awkwardness about the fact that Melissa had sucked Jack's cock and swallowed his cum seemed to have been dismissed. But that fact excited both of them more than any sex they had ever had stayed in the back of their minds. Jack often caught Melissa looking at his pants, and she often saw him gazing at her tits or legs in the short dresses the aliens provided.

It started with the feelings. Without

warning, Jack and Melissa were hit with a barrage of strobe lights. Nothing frightening had happened for hours, so when the lights dropped and the bolts came from every part of the room hitting the couple, all they could do is hold on to each other and scream.

When the bolts stopped, the lights were down and the lamps in the room on. Jack felt tingling all over his body, as did Melissa. It felt like her blood was boiling in her body. Every extremity was alive with feelings. When she looked over at Jack, her arousal took her over like she was having a medical emergency.

"What is happening to me Jack?"

She gasped crawling on the floor. Jack was pinned against the bed overcome with stimulation as well. His cock was harder than he had felt it in a long time. As he rolled his head around to gather his wits, in the darkened room, he saw the alien figures staring down at them from the windows above. They seemed larger than before, and they were pointing and they seemed to be working computers.

"Melissa, we have to fight this together."

He gasped. But they could not fight it. The video monitor came on with the image they were worried would be next. The couple on the screen was fucking with a wild passion. The spotlight landed on Melissa who was on her hands and knees on the ground. The alien voice came over the loudspeaker and Jack felt a mild jolt to the metal bands in his wrists. Just then, Melissa cried out and fell to her elbows with her butt sticking up. She had felt jolts to her torture bands too.

"Jack they want us to fuck. They are going to hurt you if we don't."

Jack was already moving his hands to push down his pants and tear off his shirt. The drugs in their systems had made them horny to the point of madness. The strobes, the jolts, and the commands all drove Jack and Melissa toward each other to do what they never thought they would ever do. Jack was going to fuck his best friend since childhood.

Jack dropped to his knees behind Melissa and pulled her skirt up over her cotton panties. He thrust his fingers into her pussy. She was soaking wet.

"Oh God Melissa, you are so sexy."

"Take me Jack. All of me."

She reached back and started pushing her panties down to just above her knees. Jack rose up on his knees to finish pushing his underwear down. Melissa's eyes grew wide with want when his big hard cock popped out ready to penetrate her. She turned over on her back to spread her legs wide to take that cock inside her cunt.

They were so eager to fuck that they didn't even get on the bed. The lights changed and the music came on showing that their tormentors were getting what they wanted. Jack lowered himself onto his beautiful best friend holding himself up by one arm to watch himself fit the head of his cock in the slit of her sweet pussy. Melissa reached under her brown thigh and held open the slit so Jack could easily match the head of his wet cock to the opening of her vagina.

Jack pushed and the rim of her pussy stretched around that big tip and he began to go inside her. Melissa gasped at the feeling of being entered, and then suddenly, the head popped inside her tight hole. Jack let out a primal groan and leaned forward pushing that stiff rod deeper and deeper inside her.

Melissa pulled him down to her when she felt him inside her and arched up to him. Jack unzipped her dress in back and pulled it down burying his face in her neck kissing and sucking it. His big cock pushed deeper into her tight insides as he pulled down her bra and kissed her tits lovingly but full of want.

"Oh yes," she whispered pushing her bosoms up to him until she felt his mouth close over her nipple and begin to suck it.

Melissa let her body fit into his shape as he fucked into her pussy again and again. With each thrust, his big cock went deeper until she could take the entire nine inches inside her. He was gasping and grunting with the excitement of fucking his sexy BFF. Suddenly, he surged into her harder than ever. "Yes baby," she whispered to encourage him, and that was all it took. He came into her doubling over with the stress and ecstasy of orgasm inside of Melissa.

Escape

It seemed like the aliens stopped paying

attention once Jack finished fucking Melissa, and they were laying there in a pile. The lights came up, the music went off and some food appeared. As both lovers returned to their rooms to freshen up, Jack leaned over and whispered to Melissa, "Only eat the fruit and fresh vegetables. Do not eat anything cooked and don't drink the wine." Melissa was confused, but she nodded and went into her room.

Several mornings later, Melissa noticed that Jack did not come out of his room right away. Instead, she found a slip of paper that said, "Quickly come in here and move to the right." Melissa did as she was told, and as soon as she was in his room, he grabbed her and pulled her out of the doorway so she could not be seen by the big windows the aliens used to watch them.

She felt the heat of his kiss.

"Melissa," Jack said. "No drugs, no beams, no torture makes me say this. I am in love with you. All I think about is how much I want to fuck you."

"I feel the same way my love. You are so exciting."

"Now listen, take these crude sunglasses I made from some material under one of my chairs. That will block the beams. The drugs are out of our system now. In a minute, we will go out to the big bed in the torture room. I am going to make love to you there. But it will not be them making it happen, it will be me. But keep your clothes on through the whole thing because we are going to escape. Just follow my lead."

The two lovers walked out of Jack's room holding hands. Instantly, the aliens appeared in the windows and the sound of alien orders started. Jack paid no attention and took Melissa to the bed and kissed her passionately. She kissed him back and pulled him down on the bed.

Suddenly, the lights went down and the beams shot out toward them. The glasses stopped any influence. Within seconds, the torture bracelets started heating up.

"Quickly, Melissa. Put the latch of your bracelet against the latch of mine. She was confused but she did was he said. In a surge, a massive jolt of power hit the bracelets. But instead of shocking the lovers, the bracelets fired that jolt into the latch of the other bracelet. All four bracelets exploded at the latch and they fell free.

"Jack fuck me. Fuck me in a way they never wanted us to fuck."

She felt powerful and free.

"I want to fuck you in the ass my love."

Jack moaned pulled her panties to the side from under her skirt. But neither of them took anything off.

"Yes Jack; put your big cock in my butt!"

Jack pushed her sexy thighs up which rolled her sweet round butt cheeks up to him. Jack looked down as Melissa grabbed each cheek and pulled her butt crack open. In one movement, Jack thrust two fingers into her pussy hole pulling them out covered with wet. He lubricated his hard cock that was sticking out of his pants with her wet and then repeated the thrust and lubricate several times each time making Melissa squeal with delight and desire.

Jack looked down at Melissa's sweet butt hole, and he smeared some her wet in that puckered opening. Without hesitation, he held her panties to the side and fit the head of his cock in her anal rim. Pressing patiently but firmly that tight virgin hole yielded to her lover. Melissa moaned and gasped at the pain of feeling Jack go up her ass. But she did not stop him because he wanted him in every hole she had.

Suddenly, the rim of her rectum yielded and opened up to Jack and his cock pushed inside her butt. Jack leaned on his arms looked down that the strain in the face of his adorable lover and feeling the tightness of her ass suck his cock. He began to thrust when it was just a few inches in. Each thrust took it further inside her. Jack was so aroused that in seconds he shot his load filling her rectum with huge streams of gooey white cum.

When Melissa felt the heat of that flood of cum fill her anal tunnel, she orgasmed hard. Both lovers moaned and shouted out their love for each other as they came defiantly showing the aliens that they belonged to each other only now.

Suddenly, the lights came up. The sounds of machines died out and the entire complex seemed to go dead. Jack pulled his cock out of Melissa's insides and sat on the bed putting himself back together. As he scanned the room, he saw it. A door suddenly opened up that was never there before.

"Now Melissa," he shouted and he pulled her from the bed. He pulled her with him across the room and out that door to freedom.

As soon as they were out, Jack was stunned to see they were not on a foreign planet. The big building that was their prison was right behind the Nostromo restaurant. It was daytime on earth, and Jack and Melissa ran toward the parking lot where their car was. Their clothes almost shredded from their latest fucking and gasping to others as they walked toward the restaurant for lunch that they should not go in there because they would be abducted by aliens and used in sex experiments.

Epilogue

The big sterile-looking rooms where the aliens tortured Jack and Melissa stood empty as the two best friends left their captivity as lovers. Just then a door that was not visible from the inside the room opened. Three strange figures came out. They did not resemble the aliens that Jack and Melissa saw conducting their experiments on those screens. They look like humans, because in fact, that is what they were. The three men moved across the room taking their lab coats off and hanging them up.

"That was awesome," one of them remarked.

"It was amazing Jim. They really believed they had been abducted, just like the two college girls. This set-up rocks. Those images of aliens scared the shit out of those kids. Where did you get them?" a second scientist responded.

"It's stock footage from some cheesy horror film," Jim answered. "It was that wine that really took over. That shit really had them seeing visions," he observed.

"More than that," the other scientist added, "It made them horny as hell. Melissa would have fucked even you, Jim; she was so loopy from those chemicals," he laughed.

"Let me borrow some of that for my wife," Jim joked.

"That was so hot, especially when Jack fucked his best friend up the ass," the first scientist remembered.

"I think the college girls we turned into lesbians were better," the other added.

"Maybe we should abduct them all and mix and match all four of them up," the first scientist joked.

"Hell, we would be here for months. We might kill them if we tried that," the second one gasped.

"That is a chance I am willing to take. Hey, who is up for a beer? I'm buying."

"You're on big guy," they all responded eagerly and they left their experimental facilities quiet at least for now.

10 KILLING TIME IN PARADISE

Working Vacation

Scarlet woke up alone in the swanky Paris hotel room. Her husband Tommy was not there. He had brought her with him to Paris because to share the adventure. He had been a celebrity photographer for 10 years. When he landed the job to be the only photographer to work on a documentary book about the big rock band, The Bees, it was a huge opportunity to take his career to the next level, plus he got a full expense paid trip to come to Paris and stay for at least three weeks or longer all paid for by the band's promoters and the label.

Scarlet got out of the big bed and walked across the suite in only her skimpy panties and cut-off t-shirt. She felt sad and alone. At first, being together in Paris was so romantic and sexy. But once the rehearsals for the new album began, Tommy was gone more and more. The band travelled around France as well to do videos and stills for promotions, and he had to go on those alone. So Scarlet had to stay in the hotel alone.

She looked in the mirror. She had no makeup on; still she was a stunningly beautiful woman. At 23, she was shapely from head to toe. Her body was round but not plump. Her lips were full and sexy, and she had a heart-stopping smile. Her breasts were not huge, but they were full and they always drew the gaze of men even from across a room. She knew she could get any man in the hotel if she wanted to, but she was a devoted wife and avoided men that she knew wanted in her panties.

Scarlet walked out and sat in the big windowsill that looked across to the big balcony that came with the room. She had little on, but it was the 69th floor of the swanky hotel, and there were no other buildings that could see in. Scarlet could see some of the other balconies on her floor too. An older couple was having tea on their balcony. Just then, Scarlet recognized the man about two doors down. She picked up a small pair of binoculars and looked him. She was certain it was Leo Castelle. It made Scarlet smile to see the international star of dozens of movies and winner of three academy awards looking out over Paris in his pajamas.

Scarlet got dressed lazily. She had no place to go and she felt lonely without her sweet and sexy husband Tommy to jump all over. Sitting on the bed wearing only her blouse, she thought of that night they checked into this room. Tommy was so excited he just threw money at the bellhop to get her alone.

As she thought of that afternoon, Scarlet let her fingers slip into her panties. She remembered how she had arrived wearing her traveling outfit, a pretty yellow dress that was light and loose on her. As soon as the bellhop was out the door, Tommy rushed to her from behind with such lust that she squealed with excitement. She felt his mouth on her neck sucking, kissing, and biting it. His hands slid under her arms and landed on her tits squeezing them through the thin fabric of the dress. Scarlet was standing the edge of the bed so she pushed her knees into the mattress and bent a little to let him know that what she was his for the taking.

"Oh God baby," Tommy moaned sucking his sexy wife's earlobe. "Look at this place. This is the perfect place for our first fuck in Paris." Scarlet just moaned and arched her head back to let him taste her skin because she liked that phrase "first fuck." It meant there were to be many more fucks.

As Scarlet remembered that first exciting sex in that hotel room, she slid her fingers over her clit missing her husband badly. Her eyes were closed and her other hand was on her right tit rubbing it and stimulating the hard nipple under her light cut-off t-shirt. She felt her hips thrusting up to her finger with that strong fucking motion that she felt into each time Tommy pushed his sweet cock inside her.

Scarlet remembered her excitement as Tommy bent her over the bed pulling up her skirt. She felt so taken and sexy as he slid her panties down and didn't even take the time to take them off. He left them at her knees as he fell on her pushing his pants down to let his hard cock out. He was so eager to fuck her; he didn't even take the time to get clothing off.

Scarlet grabbed the covers and bunched them up in her hands as she felt her husband squeezing her ass cheeks. Tommy did not have a large cock, but he was demanding and lustful when he fucked his gorgeous wife and that excited Scarlet. She loved that feeling of being wanted and taken by the man she adored. He mounted her and his mouth began to suck and bite her neck, shoulder, and back.

Just then Scarlet felt his cock drive inside her dripping wet pussy hole. "Oh baby, I love being inside of you," he moaned as he began to fuck her with long deep thrusts. "Fuck me Tommy," was all that Scarlet could moan as she lifted her ass to her husband so he could drive deeper into her wet cunt. As Scarlet remembered that feeling of Tommy's hard cock deep in her, she thrust two fingers inside herself and began to fuck in and out of her vagina.

She remembered his arms around her stomach holding on as he fucked her like an animal. His fingers grasped and squeezed her sensitive tits. Scarlet moaned with lust being molested so roughly by the man she loved. The relentless fucking in and out got faster and more demeaning, and Scarlet pushed back with her hips and thighs to get his eager cock deeper in her. Then like they were one organism, Scarlet came hard falling to her face in the bed just as Tommy emptied a huge load of cum inside her.

"Oh My God," Scarlet cried out all by herself in that hotel room. She arched up to her own fingers and felt the rush of her orgasm fill her body. And then she fell limp. She felt satisfied but alone and sad at the same time. She got up and took a shower.

Playfulness

Leo was not impressed with the luxury suite the sponsors of his trip had provided. He had plenty of money from his dozens and dozens of hit movies over the years. The life of a celebrity was tiring and lonely. The public did not know that. This trip to Paris was not something he really wanted to do. It was just for some appearances and promotional photography and a few commercials for his French fans. It was good pay; the accountants worried about that.

Because of his fame, Leo was used to throngs of fans running after him. The hotel he was in was good about keeping that to a minimum. They did all they could to make his stay luxurious and enjoyable. But they could not cut the aching loneliness that he felt from being away from his wife and his two daughters. Each night after dinner, he called his wife Elaine and talked to her. He wanted to tell how much he wanted her in his bed there in Paris. He wanted her to know that his cock ached to be inside her. But she just talked about her plans to remodel the kitchen or the hundred other ways she was spending his vast amount of money he had earned.

It got to where one of his favorite parts of his day was coffee on the terrace and that was because he often saw that pretty young woman two terraces down. What he did not know is that the young woman he noticed on her terrace was Scarlet, and with her husband away day after day, those moments eye flirting with the famous movie star were important to her too. Those mornings started out simple. Scarlet and Leo sat on their terraces looking out at Paris. She would look over to see if he was looking only to see his head turn suddenly. Amused she would stare at him until his head turned suddenly and she snapped her gaze away pretending not to be looking. Then the movie star would stare back at her and she would turn only to see him look away.

After three days of this, Scarlet stepped out onto the terrace wearing the big white terrycloth robe the hotel provided. When Leo began to come out, he spotted her wearing that, and he slipped back inside and stripped down to nothing and put on the same robe. When he stepped out, he stretched with his arms wide open and the robe opened but he was facing forward. That was all it took. The young wife burst out laughing and the sound of her laughter was like music to the lonely movie star. It made him laugh out loud too and the pretense of being strangers was destroyed.

She turned with her robe securely closed and smiled over to the older man. But Leo was bent over the little table writing on a piece of cardboard. He held up a sign to her that just said. "I am Leo." Scarlet giggled and quickly found a marker and a piece of cardboard of her own and then held it up to simply say, "I know." Leo laughed loudly at her answer. He was also captivated when she flipped over her card and wrote, "I am Scarlet" on it. He followed her lead and created a new sign of her own on the back that just said, "I Know!" That was all it took and she ran into the suite giggling.

The day for Leo was tedious as he went about the business of being the star and smiling for the cameras. Much of the work was in the hotel, and while he was doing a photo shoot near the bar, he spotted Scarlet watching him from the back of the crowd. When he thought nobody was looking, he stuck his tongue out at her. He got away with it, but when she poked her head around, a tall crewmember returned the gesture and he cracked up. He also noticed she had an adorable tongue.

The Fan

Leo felt tired and alone. The day was behind him. The manager of the Paris schedule called and offered him a whore. For the first week, that was an acceptable compromise. At least if he shot his cum into a prostitute, he could sleep. But soon, the ugliness of paying a woman to take his cock was too much for him. It was even worse than those times when he let groupies who were in awe of his celebrity into his bed where he would fuck them and throw them away. Deep inside Leo was a good person. He hated treating women like that.

There was a VIP bar in the hotel. That was a good place to go because not everybody had access to it. It got him out of the room and sometimes someone who admired his work bought him his drink. Leo had almost gotten to the point of fearing being recognized and feeling hostile toward the public that had made him a success. But he always accepted the drinks.

As he sat alone at the bar, he thought about the cute young woman who was on the same floor of the hotel with him. The fun of "flirting" with her was nothing but that. There was nothing ugly or dirty about it. Of course, he could easily see that Scarlet was a gorgeous and very sexy young woman, but he was old enough to be her father and it was enough that she made him smile. Even as he nursed his martini, he missed her.

Suddenly, Leo heard the sound of female voices. He looked out into the lobby area and there was a gathering of middle-aged women. A woman's club from Topeka Kansas was enjoying a trip to Paris, and they were getting together for the sightseeing trip. The giggling and chatter about the excitement of the trip filled the lower half of the hotel. Leo watched them with amusement, but just then, he spotted Scarlet on the other side of the throng. She turned and saw him and stuck her tongue out at him. Before he could react, she disappeared out the door into the Paris streets. But he had stood and moved toward the bar entrance to try to connect with her.

Before he could pull back from the group, one of the women turned around and recognized him. Heather was a mother of two whose husband was the pastor of the Topeka First Baptist Church. The rest of the women were moving toward the door where there was a bus waiting for their tour. "Oh my God," Heather whispered looking right up at the movie star that she adored from afar for so long. "You are Leo Castelle!"

Before she could get out of the whisper range, Leo put his finger on her lips to hush her. He did not want to have a rush of fans overwhelm him especially in the mood he was in. Heather did hush and followed her screen idol into the bar as the crooking of his finger. Leo hardly ever "played" with a fan like this anymore. He did not mean to play with Heather, but she did not turn into the screaming teenager as so many of his fans did. It was not hard to notice that for a suburban Kansas mom of two kids, she was quite a beautiful woman. Her long black hair shaped her face like a picture frame. She was not slender, but she was round in all the right places. Her breasts were noticeably plump and inviting, and while her hips had a little middle-aged spread, her legs that were showing below her stylish skirt were very sexy.

Heather did behave like a schoolgirl when she first came into the bar. She was full of so many questions, and she was shocked that Leo was so patient in answering them. Suddenly, she realized that she had missed her bus and the other women. Leo asked her if she wanted to try to catch up with them, but she was not going to miss out on being with a handsome and sexy movie star Leo; she helped him feel less lonely although he remembered how often he had exploited fans.

"Would you like a drink?" Leo offered, putting his hand on her knee. She accepted even though she hardly ever drank. As a minister's wife, she was shocked to find herself in a Paris bar with a handsome movie star giving her alcohol and feeling her knee. She felt nervous and a little frightened but turned on way she had not experienced before. She was more than flattered. She wanted to walk on the wild side if that was what this was.

Leo looked the beautiful Midwestern mom up and down and felt his want for her body take over. He knew it was wrong, but he wanted her in his bed to use her admiration for him to overcome her morals and fuck him until he felt done. The drink went right to her head, and she was chattering a mile a minute as she felt the handsome movie star push his hand under her skirt and begin to feel the soft skin of her upper thighs.

"Oh," she said with her voice suddenly

soft and shy. “My husband feels me there.” When she looked Leo in the eyes, he kissed her deeply. She felt those fingers go higher and find her cotton panties exploring the fabric just barely covering her pussy. “I shouldn’t,” she whispered as he kissed her neck, but she was his for the taking.

Leo stood and paid for the drinks. Taking her hand, he guided her to a private elevator from the VIP bar that went to the floor where the luxury suites were. Heather followed him into that elevator, and as it took them up the tower of the hotel, he slipped his arms around her from behind and kissed and sucked her neck. Her heart was racing, and in spite of herself, she felt her pussy getting very wet.

Inside his luxurious suite, Heather was overwhelmed with the exotic and exciting thing that was happening to her. Leo sat her on the bed and knelt on the floor in front of her calmly undoing the buttons of her blouse. “I am married and a Christian woman,” she whispered as she watched him pull open her top. He was so smooth, and she could see the lust in his eyes. That look had vanished from her marriage long ago.

“Are you excited?” Leo said in a low sexy voice. He pushed her blouse over her arms leaning in and kissing her shoulder and neck.

“Oh God. It’s so wrong, but yes, I am so excited,” she said just as he undid her bra. He kissed her mouth driving his tongue into her lips. Pulling her bra free, her wide tits fall apart from each other. Leo leaned down and found one of her nipples and licked it. It was wide, red, and stiff with arousal. Heather moaned pulling the blankets off of the bed with her fists, pushing her tits up to him.

As Leo sucked her sexy tit, he hooked his arms in behind her knees and pushed her legs up and apart and pushed her back onto the bed so she was lying on her back. “Oh God Leo,” she gasped as she felt her legs pushed apart and her skirt push up above her thighs. Leo moved over and sucked the other nipple deep in his mouth as he stroked up and down those wide thighs enjoying the soft smoothness of her skin.

“Do you want me to fuck you, Heather?” he said softly. She was shocked by the swear word and driven to insane levels of lust by it too.

“Oh god yes, it’s so wrong but fuck me deep Leo,” she gasped. In a smooth motion, Leo unzipped his pants and pulled out his long hard cock. He took her soft hand and placed it on his shaft as he pulled aside the soaking wet crotch of her panties. Heather felt up and down it and thought it would never end. It was so much bigger than her preacher husband’s tiny cock and much harder than she thought they could get. He was going to stretch her inside for sure.

Leo moved his hard cock to her cunt as his other hand pushed open the soft folds of her pussy lips. She pushed up to him as he continued pushing her tits into his chest as she felt the head push inside her. He was the first man inside her other than her husband. Feeling the rim of her vagina stretch around that huge cock caused Heather to orgasm harder than she had ever cum before.

Leo thrust in and out of her lustily. Heather felt so violated and taken and each time she even thought about that fact that she was fucking a movie star, she came again. Leo felt her cunt constrict around him and it got to him. Oddly, just before he came, he thought of that beautiful young woman on the balcony. As his body convulsed with his orgasm, he fired a huge load of cum inside of Heather, filling the deep parts of her womanhood with his sperm.

An Intimate Friendship

Leo finished and felt the sense of relief of his balls being emptied. He did escort her back to the lobby and hugged her goodbye. He knew she would be quiet about this because having a wild fuck fling would ruin her in the eyes of the other Christian women, and it would devastate her marriage and her good husband's ministry. She would have to be satisfied her life, but she had that wildly erotic fuck with a movie star that should could never speak of, but that she would always remember.

Leo had told himself he would stop fucking fans especially nice sweet mothers and wives like Heather. But he had done it again. Over the next week, he spent more and more time with Scarlet. While she was far sexier than Heather or even his wife, the time Leo spent with her was warm, sweet, affectionate, and safe. He felt protective of her, and they were two lonely spouses separated from the husband and wife they loved.

During days when he was not working, he took Scarlet to museums, shops, and restaurants around town. They had fun watching the French and Americans try to figure out if they were lovers or if he was her dad. At one point in the elevator of a busy office building on the way up to the restaurant on top, she whispered to him just loud enough for everyone to hear, “Let’s go home and go to bed daddy.” And then she kissed his neck seductively. The gasp in the elevator was sharp, and it was all both Scarlet and Leo could do not to break out laughing.

Evenings were the loneliest and Leo had sworn off hanging out in the VIP lounge. So he and Scarlet spent the evenings in her suite or his. They ordered room service, but when it came, the visitor hid in the bathroom so they would not be seen together. Then they curled and watched a movie on the big sofa or in the bed. It was loving but never dirty. Leo cared for her.

One evening, they snuggled on the big divan watching a romantic comedy. Leo stayed with it until the end, but when it was over, he realized his beautiful friend was asleep on his chest. She was curled up into his pajamas top peacefully breathing deeply. They were in his suite and he did not want to wake her. Gently, he moved her sleeping form until he could stand and pick her up in his arms.

In her sleep, she was being held by someone dear and loving and she wrapped her arms around Leo's neck. He held her under her naked legs very aware that all she had on was a cut-off t-shirt and skimpy panties. But he felt a sense of caring for her that he treasured. He gently placed her in his bed. Looking down at her gorgeous sexy thighs, he was taken with how amazingly sexy she was.

Just then, she moved slightly making a sweet girlish hum and the crotch of her panties parted just enough that Leo got a look at the folds of her sweet pussy. He became erect looking at this delicious sexy girl in his bed. But he did not pay attention to his raging hard on. He simply leaned over and kissed her on the forehead. At that, her eyes opened slightly and she looked at him, lifted her face to his, and kissed his lips. "I love you," she said softly and went back to sleep.

That night Leo found some blankets in the closet and curled up on the big sofa and slept near the sweet girl. It was not for lack of wanting to fuck her, but he loved that sense of trust she had in him and he would not violate that. The next night, they had another movie planned at her suite. Instead of using the couch, Leo and Scarlet curled up in her bed. The thoughts of their late night kiss were in both of their minds. Once again, she only had on light panties and a cut-off top. She held him tight as the movie had some suspense, and at one point, she put her sexy leg over his middle and sensed his erection.

The movie ended, and Leo changed it to a soft music channel. She just kept holding on to him, but she was not asleep. Finally, he said softly, "I should go."

"No. I want you to stay with me." Scarlet said softly as she gazed up to his face. Leo melted as feelings for her filled him up. Without thinking, he kissed her lips. They both knew that she loved her husband and he loved his wife. But the feelings in that quiet bedroom alone in Paris were real. The kiss lasted, and there was another as their mouths opened to kiss deeply. Scarlet moaned happily at the secure feeling of being in his arms.

Leo loved Scarlet because she never cared that he was a star. Scarlet loved Leo because even walking around almost naked, she never felt he was lusting after her or there to fuck her. That was one of the reasons that in that bed, she wanted to fuck him all the more.

Leo laid her head on the soft pillow and kissed her deeply loving the taste of the inside of her mouth as his tongue searched it. She sucked his tongue lovingly. He caressed her tummy and then let his hand rub her stomach moving it up under her top. When he found her perfectly shaped breasts, he felt he would never stop loving her. At the same time, he felt her hand slide into his pajamas bottoms and begin to stroke his very hard cock.

"I have dreamed of being with you like this," she whispered.

"Me too, sweetie," he said, pulling her top over her head. "I adore you."

As his loving kisses made their way down her neck to her shoulders and then to her sexy tits, Scarlet pushed Leo's pajamas down to release his big, thick erection. He was much bigger than her husband, but she wanted him inside her so much. "I want you Leo," she whispered wiggling out of her panties. "I want you to fuck me," she said, and it drove him wild with passion hearing her angelic voice talk dirty.

Rolling on top of her, he reached under her sexy body and grasped her firm butt cheeks pulling her toward him. She opened her thighs wide to let her newest and dearest friend inside her vagina. He felt her fingers move the head of his hard cock to her wet opening so Leo braced himself on his arms so he did not crush her. When he felt the warm wetness of her pussy hole, he applied gentle pressure. Her fingers stayed on the shaft to keep the angle right so they worked together to achieve perfect penetration.

Inch by inch, Leo felt his long cock go inside the young woman's wet insides. They kissed and let their tongues be inside each other's mouths as his cock filled her pussy hole. His fucking motions started out slow to enjoy every sensation of the wall of her cunt stroking his hard cock.

"Oh God Leo, fuck me deep," Scarlet moaned kissing and sucking his neck. Leo began to pound his hard manhood into the young girl's very wet cunt again and again and again. "OH LEO," Scarlet gasped, cumming hard as she took the entire length of his huge cock that stretched the inside of her cunt. He pushed up looking down on the sexy naked body of this girl he adored. Then he came filling her with his hot cum in huge spurts inside her.

They fucked often in the last week before they left. When it was time for him to go back to Hollywood, he held her and kissed her. "I don't want to lose you," she wept holding his frame possessively.

"You won't," he said pressing a business card into her hand that had a special cell phone number on it that was only for her. "You are in my heart and that is a living thing in me forever," he said kissing her and getting into the limo. What he did not know is that a living thing that was part of him was in her and that was the tiny baby that came from their lovemaking.

11 SUDDENLY SUBMISSIVE

Strange Encounter

Carly had been to the grocery store. It was a hot day in June and after she dropped her two children off at their day camps for the day, she had time to get some chores done. One thing she liked about summer is seeing the neighborhood kids playing in the cul-du-sac or frolicking in their sprinklers in their front yards. As she pulled out of her driveway, Brad, the neighbor's son, was shooting baskets in a hoop his dad had put up facing the end of the street where their houses were. She rolled down the window to greet him. He had always been a good kid.

"Hi Brad. What are you doing this summer?" she said cheerfully.

"Hi, Mrs. Jordon. Oh, I'm just working for my dad and doing odd jobs around the neighborhood. I graduated high school so I will be heading off to state college in the fall."

"Congratulations!" Carly said sincerely. "I had no idea you were that far along in school," she continued.

"Well I am 18 now so its time I get after it," the handsome boy said laughing. "So if you need your lawn mowed or any chores done, I am here until September," he said promoting himself.

Carly laughed and admired at what a handsome boy he had become. Along with handsome, it did not escape her notice that he was big, muscular, and sexy in that young man sort of way. "Well I do need some chores done tomorrow so you come by about 10 after I drop Missy and Jimmy off at day camp," she instructed the boy.

"Will do Mrs. Jordon," he answered happily sinking a basket and smiling broadly. Carly parked the car in front of her house because she would need to go run some errands in a little while. She started to get the groceries out when she heard the phone ringing in the house. She ran in and handled the call, and when she came out, she noticed that Brad was still shooting baskets but he had taken of his shirt. She gasped at the rippling muscles on the boy's body. She had known Brad since he and his parents moved into the cul-de-sac when he was six. Admiring and getting excited at his body seemed quite wrong.

Carly walked to the car watching that sexy boy and trying not to be too conspicuous. She opened the back door that faced the street and took a bag of kitchen supplies out of the car. Suddenly, the basketball Brad was shooting bounced hard off of the backboard of the goal and flew toward the car. It hit the door of the car and ricocheted into the groceries knocking them out of Carly's hands so they spilled all over the street.

Brad ran over embarrassed and fell to the pavement picking up the spilled groceries and apologizing. Carly felt a flush seeing that sexy body bent at her feet so she stepped away so he would not notice she was blushing and looking at his back muscles and his firm and powerful legs. She trotted over to where the ball came to rest and playfully tossed it toward Brad saying in her light and feminine voice, "Catch, Brad."

But Brad did not hear her. The ball grazed his temple and bounced back into the street. Suddenly, Brad felt his temper come up like it did when he used to play ball with his cousin. He turned his face toward Carly with a passionate anger in his eyes. "What did you do?" he said demandingly. "You are so STUPID!" he said forgetting himself. "NOW GET ME THAT BALL!"

Carly was overpowered by his demands and she ran and got the ball. Just as suddenly, her body was flushed with a warm surge of excitement. She felt weak in the knees and a strange tingling in her nipples and pussy. "Yes, Brad" she found herself saying softly lowering her face to look down as she brought the ball to him.

"NOW GO GET ME A COKE," he demanded throwing the groceries into the car and slamming the door. He turned toward the pretty young housewife and Carly noticed that in his cut-off jeans, he had a hard-on.

"Yes Brad," she softly obeyed and she ran as best she could up the driveway and into the house. Once inside, she fell to her knees to the carpet gasping like she was having a medical attack. "Oh god, what is happening to me?" she whispered to herself.

Carly felt out of control. Feeling like her pussy was about to explode she pulled up her skirt in full view of the window to the street. She saw the sexy boy finishing the cleanup at the car, his muscles shimmering in the sunlight. She thrust her fingers into her panties and found her cunt oozing wet more than when she had sex with her husband. She thrust two fingers into her wet pussy hole and thrust them in and out just three times. Suddenly, she gasped out loud and then an orgasm hit with a power she had never known.

Nubian Neighbor

Brad was overwhelmed with shame that he had acted so rudely toward Mrs. Jordon. When she did not come out, he gathered the groceries into the bag that was not broken too bad and carried it to the door and left it there. He put a note on the top that just read, "I'm so sorry Mrs. Jordon," and he signed it. The last thing he wanted was for his parents to hear about his temper tantrum toward a neighbor that everyone in the neighborhood really liked.

Brad went into the house to calm down. He decided to do some gardening that his mom had been bothering him about. Getting a chore done would make him like less of a creep for yelling at the neighbor. But as he worked outside, he kept thinking about how she responded with her face down and that submissive “Yes Brad” answer. He also thought about the huge hard-on he got yelling at her. But at the same time, he hoped she did not tell her husband which would result in him getting in a lot of trouble.

Brad worked in just his tight shorts and sneakers without socks so he could get plenty of sun and work on his tan. His house was two doors down from the Jordon’s. The house between them had just been sold and a nice young couple moved into it. They were a black couple and they did not have any children. Brad had met them when his mom took them some cookies to welcome them to the neighborhood. His name was Leo Franklin and her name was Georgia. From the chats around the table, Brad learned that Leo was in his 30s but Georgia was just 23.

As Brad was walking a bag of trash toward the area where it was stacked, he heard sounds from the yard of the new neighbors. When he walked out, he saw Georgia working in her yard. She looked amazing to him and he just then realized how sexy she was. She had a delicate build but it was round and feminine. Her skin was a gorgeous deep dark shade like dark chocolate. She only had on a short pair of white shorts so that it showed off her sexy black thighs beautifully. Her breasts were not large but they stood out because she was so tiny.

"Hi," Brad called out and the big smile that spread on her face was adorable.

"Hi Brad!" she yelled across the back yards. "I am Georgia. We met when your mom brought over cookies. They were delicious!" she said with a cute giggle.

"I remember" he called back admiring her sexy hips and neck and turning so his slight erection did not show. Both of them returned to their work but Brad could hear the sweet wife singing softly as she worked on her flowers. That house had a lot of beds around the edge of the yard so it would take plenty of work to make them look good.

Brad almost forgot the sexy black neighbor was over there until he heard her gasp and make sounds like she was struggling. He ran toward the short ornamental fence between yards and saw Georgia struggling with a big tree branch that had fallen into her beds. It was heavy and she was having trouble with it.

"Mrs. Franklin, can I help you with that?" he cried out. Georgia looked over and just then noticed the rippling muscles on the big handsome white boy.

"Oh yes Brad that would be wonderful," she answered. Brad opened the little gate, let himself into the yard, and approached that branch with determination. He wrestled it up onto his shoulder to carry it to the side yard where her husband could cut it up to go into the trash. But for a moment, he lost balance and it fell off of him and topped into the green grass of Georgia's yard. Brad was not hurt but he did drop onto the ground to guide the load down and for a moment, he was on his butt next to it.

Georgia ran over in a panic. "Oh my god Brad, are you ok?" she said almost crying from concern. Brad tried to stand and lift the big branch but it was awkward and it rolled away which caused Brad to dip toward it. As he did that, his hand reached out toward Georgia. The tiny woman tried to grab that big muscular arm but his fingers suddenly got a hold of the front of her tiny work blouse. Before either knew it, Brad had pulled down Georgia's blouse and her beautiful perfectly rounded tits were exposed to him.

Both Brad and Georgia froze but Brad's strong fist was pulling down his neighbor woman's top without giving up. Brad stared at those sexy round tits feeling his hard-on begin to push against his shorts. Her nipples were darker than the surrounding skin and the nipples stuck out because in spite of herself, Georgia was suddenly very aroused.

Georgia tried to gather her thoughts but the lustful gaze of the muscular boy on her tits had her dizzy with desire and fear. Without thinking, Brad moved his hand from the fabric of her top to those mounds of sexy flesh on her chest. He passed his finger over her tits rubbing and massaging the nipples as he had so often with high school girls he had fucked. As had happened earlier, his passions overcame his good sense.

Georgia felt her heart beating in her ears. She felt her body on fire with lust for this sexy young guy in her yard. But she had only been married for a year and was madly in love with Leo. Cheating was out of the question. As Brad felt her tits, she tried to move. “Brad, I don’t think....” She started to say as she moved to stand up. But as she did, she put her hand out to stabilize herself and it landed on his crotch with the fingers wrapped around the shape of Brad’s big hard cock in his shorts.

When Brad felt that sweet hand on his cock through his shorts, instinct kicked in. He leaned into Georgia pulling her down onto the grass as he released his fly and snap. Georgia hardly had time to react feeling that muscular man taking her in her own yard. It was both scary and very exciting. He felt Brad’s lips find her neck sucking it and his hands pushing her onto her back. At the same time, that hand that felt fabric was now holding the young man’s big hard cock. It was as big as her husband and that instinct made her start stroking it up and down. That only encouraged Brad to fuck the beautiful black neighbor woman in her own back yard.

“No Brad, it’s wrong,” she moaned but when his lips pressed onto hers, she opened them wide kissing back hard and sucking his tongue as it slid into her mouth. She glanced down at that big white cock and the surge of lust in her took her over too. Brad wiggled out of his shorts and got on his knees. He rolled the young wife on her back and pulled her shorts down. Georgia knew this was against her morals in every way but that big muscular boy wanted to fuck her so bad and her cunt was oozing wet to be fucked.

Pushing those sexy black legs apart, Brad looked with lust at the first black pussy he had ever seen as he prepared to fuck. Pushing those thighs apart, he leaned in and then kissed her right tit letting that sweet sexy nipple enter his mouth. Georgia moaned feeling her nipple being sucked and chewed and threw her legs wide open to take his cock inside her.

As Brad's mouth moved to her other tit, Georgia felt a cock that was not her husband's find her very wet pussy hole. He pushed open her sensitive pussy lips and began to enter her. Georgia pushed up and wrapped her arms around that muscular neck letting her instinct to fuck back kick in. As Brad began to pump his big cock in and out of her, she thrust back trying to take it all deep in her. On the green grass of her back yard, her gorgeous black body rolled in dirty passion with the son of her neighbor's, fucking and kissing him back. And when Brad suddenly gasped and shot his load inside her, she just held onto him and thrust back more until she came all over that big white hard-on.

Taking Care of Mrs. Jordon

Brad showed up at Carly's house the next day ready to do yard work for her. He had the gorgeous black beauty that lived between the Carly's house and his on his mind all night long. But he vowed to behave respectfully at Mrs. Jordon's after that mess where he yelled at her. He wore some clean jeans shorts and a longer top, but he had to go with little on because it would be so hot to work. Carly got him working quickly and their relationship was warm and sweet as it had always been. They both assumed the incident was not a big deal.

After a while, Brad saw Mrs. Jordon come out on her patio to take care of some of the flowers in planters. He glanced at her body and how shapely it was. She was not tiny and slender like Georgia's but was sexy in her own way, and her butt was round and her thighs were full. She wore her brownish red hair in a short cut so that the ends curled under her chin. Her face was cute and sweet which always brought smiles to the faces of people she met. It was a wholesome look that did not fit someone who masturbated on the floor of her entry hall watching a young boy as she had done the previous day.

Carly wore white shorts and a flowered top. It was open on top so she could get sun on her shoulders and chest but she did have a bra on, as she was being careful around a young guy whose hormones had control. It was a hot day and before long, Brad had peeled off his shirt revealing the contours of his very muscular chest, arms, shoulders, and back. Brad noticed Carly glancing over at him and that stirred him inside with that feeling that drove him to crawl on top of his sweet black neighbor woman and fuck her hard the day before.

Finally, after working about an hour, Brad stopped and stood up and said more to himself than to Mrs. Jordon, "I'm thirsty." Carly heard him from the deck. As she stood up, Brad looked at her. He had a strange look in his eye.

"Get me a coke now!" he said commandingly in that same tone he used the day before except firm and not angry. When he said that, Carly did not move at first. She looked like she had been slapped and at first Brad thought that what happened in the street was a fluke and she was going to get mad. Instead, suddenly her face lowered and she said softly.

"Yes Brad." Carly walked back into the kitchen with her mind and body flooding with feelings. Why was she acting like this? What makes me have to obey him? Why is my pussy on fire when he orders me like this? There were no answers. She got the drinks and took them on the patio where Brad had laid down in a lounge chair with his arms out like a king. She handed the soda too him blushing and looking down.

"Kneel before me," he commanded. Now

he was getting out of line. And yet, Carly obeyed. She got on her knees and the wood of the deck hurt her skin. She bowed to him and handed the drink up to him. Brad looked at the sexy suburban mom kneeling before him and he liked it. His erection bulged his work shorts out.

"Look at me," he commanded Carly. Carly lifted her head and her eyes were wet. She was emotional along with wild desire coming from this sudden submissive side of her. "Look at my pants," Brad ordered her. Carly gazed at the huge bulge in his pants. "What do you see?" Brad ordered her to tell him.

"You have a hard-on," she answered blushing horribly.

"Do you want to see my cock?" he said sternly to her. Carly just nodded not knowing what else to do. She thought of her husband and kids and here she was feeling an overpowering need to see and touch and do much more with this young guys cock. "Say it slave!" he demanded.

"I want to see your cock Brad," Carly said choking on the words.

"Take it out of my pants," he ordered her. Carly was shocked and the blush that took her over felt fatal to her. But the submissive Carly would not dare to disobey. She leaned forward as Brad opened his legs. She put her hands on his hairy thighs feeling her way up them. The firm young muscles of his legs excited her.

Slowly she unzipped his pants until his underwear appeared. Then she reached in and pulled the underwear down. The massive bulge of Brad's hard cock made it hard to get the underwear over it. When it did move, that huge stiff cock sprang out above his legs. It was easily twice the size of her husband's cock. "Oh god," Carly said, gazing at it and feeling her insides yearn for that huge penis to drill her deep.

Carly caressed that beautiful cock up and down and within moments, an ooze of pre-cum emerged from the tip. Then Carly moved her soft hands down to his big teenage boy balls and caressed them too. "Mmmm," Brad hummed in pleasure. "Is your husband's cock as sexy as mine?" he teased her.

"No Brad," she whispered only feeling a mixture of guilt and excitement at cheating with the neighbor boy as his sex slave.

"Suck my cock Mrs. Jordon," Brad commanded. He sounded so respectful with his obscene command. But Carly was far too far gone to stop now. She rarely sucked her husband's cock because he was the kind who got on, fucked a short time, shot, and fell off. But Carly leaned forward, licked Brad's big cock and then put it in her mouth. "Hold your head still and suck," he commanded her and then Brad reached down and grasped the sides of her face holding her soft hair in his hands.

Brad began to fuck into her mouth faster and faster. Carly tried to hold on feeling that stiff member thrust into her mouth, slide over her tongue, and back out again. The salty and pungent taste of his genitals and moisture filled her mouth and nose. "Oh god," Brad said thrusting deeper into her mouth and almost choking her. "I am going to cum," he said.

Carly panicked about his putting his cum in her mouth. He felt her pulling. Suddenly he was not harsh or demanding but comforting. "It's ok Mrs. Jordon. Hold the vein under my cock. Let it spurt the cum on your tongue and drink it as you can. It won't hurt you," he said gasping at his fast coming orgasm.

Then it hit. A huge surge of hot cum shot into her mouth. Quickly Carly did as Brad said and pressed the vein to stop the flow. She could not think of anything to do because his big hard prick filled her mouth up and it was oozing cum like a flood. She released the vein and more shot in and she closed it and swallowed over and over again. Finally the flow stopped. Carly released his cock and drank some soda to cleanse her mouth and throat.

Carly stood up and walked to the railing around the deck. She leaned on it shaking. Then she heard Brad stand up. She hoped this whole master submission thing was over now that she had sucked his hard cock and swallowed all of his sperm. But unlike her husband, one-time cumming was not enough. Brad looked at the sexy wife and mother of two and he got hard again right away.

Carly heard Brad walking and then the sound of his pants falling to the wood panels of the deck. Then he was behind her pressing against her back. He leaned in and whispered in her ear. “You are wet for me?” he hissed in her ear.

“Yes Brad,” she said in her submissive tone.

“My cock is bigger than your husband’s?” he said wanting to hear it again.

“Lots bigger Brad,” she answered truthfully.

“You want to feel it in your cunt?” he said obscenely in her ear.

“I do Brad,” she confessed hating the slut that he had turned her into.

This time he did not just command her to do all the work. “Lean forward,” he commanded as she leaned on her hands as she felt his fingers push her shorts down. They slid over her the round cheeks of her ass and dropped down her sexy thighs. Carly arched her butt back and that is when she felt Brads hard cock press into the folds of her butt. She was stunned how hard it was after just cumming.

Brad leaned in, kissed her neck, and bit her on the earlobe and that pain made Carly moan with pleasure. One of his eager hands ran under her top from the tummy and felt up toward her bra. The other one slid down her back and into the crack of her butt spreading and feeling every inch of that private crevasse.

Brad pushed her bra up and over her tits and began to fondle Carly’s fleshy breasts pinching the skin under each tit and then squeezing her nipples. Then he slid his hand in her ass over her butt hole pausing there to caress that opening. He found her wet and warm pussy slit and pushed the lips open finding the dripping wet opening of her vagina. His was the only finger to ever touch there besides her husband, her doctor, or herself.

"You want me to fuck you?" he said pushing his cock into the gap between her legs.

"Yes Brad," she confessed.

"Say it. Beg me," he demanded his slave woman.

"Brad I want you to fuck me. Please fuck me hard. Cum in me," Carly said, having no control over what was coming out of her mouth. She did not have to wait long to feel satisfaction. She leaned hard on the railing and opened her brown thighs apart so Brad could get his cock into the slit of her pussy. Reaching down from the front, Brad found the head of his cock and guided it to her eager hole.

"Oh god, yes," Carly said when she felt that head press the opening to her womb. In one thrust, Brad pushed inside her. Inch after inch that long and wide cock stretched Carly making her put her head back and moan so loud that many neighbors were alarmed. Brad was a wild man. He grasped her by the middle and drilled the entire length of his shaft into the deepest part of her pussy.

Then he pushed his hands up, took a tit in each hand, and squeezed as he began to fuck Mrs. Jordon feeling her cunt pull him inside her. Carly moaned feeling that huge cock stretch her like she was a virgin. Brads powerful young muscles fucked her harder than she knew was possible until she began to gasp, "yes, yes, yes" with each thrust. Every fiber of her being was fucking that 18-year-old boy, feeling his stiffness as deep inside her as anyone could go.

"I'm going to cum!" he gasped drilling the full shaft far up inside the married woman. He did not even think about pulling out. With an animal groan, Brad doubled over on top of Carly and pumped her full of his young sperm with huge spurts that seemed to drive his seed deep into her womb.

Brad left after he finally went limp inside of Carly. Both of them felt awkward. Even as he went to the back of the deck to dress, Brad got hard looking at the cute ass of that woman he had known for years and the woman he had just fucked full of cum. That is when he knew that this master-slave lust relationship was far from over. As Brad looked across the yards and saw the sexy black neighbor woman Georgia step out into her yard with her husband holding her hand, he knew it was only beginning.

12 THE TEACHER

The Henderson family drove up to the drop off area in front of the youth department at the church as they always did every Wednesday night. It was youth and family night and each week, everybody in the family had a job to do. Jim took Stevie over to the children's area where they had a full evening of fun things for those kids to do. Then usually Jim helped out the youth pastor with the physical set up of rooms and any chores related to the activities that he had planned for the middle and high school kids in the church.

Katy had just turned 18, so this was a great summer to be an intern with the middle schoolers. She was excited to be working under the handsome new youth pastor that the church had just hired. He had only been in leadership for a month and already Pastor Glen was loved by the kids and parents alike. In Katy's mind, it didn't hurt that Pastor Glen was drop-dead sexy and gorgeous, although she knew those thoughts of fucking him were so very wrong so she kept them to herself.

The youth department also had plenty of work to do for moms and that is where Mrs. Henderson had found her niche. As soon as Jim dropped Katy and her at the youth wing to take Stevie over to his activities, Amanda hugged Katy and went to the kitchen area to see how the snack preparation was coming along. For the most part the family did not see each other again until they gathered to go home after their exciting night at the church.

Katy entered the offices of the youth ministry and the two other youth interns were already there doing preparations for the evening and for the next weekend's activities. "Is Pastor Glen here yet?" Katy said to Mindy and Samantha casually.

"If he was here, don't you think Samantha would be on top of him?" Mindy said in a very catty way.

"Mindy, I don't think that is fair," Katy said sanctimoniously. "But Samantha, no more fooling around. Pastor Glen is married and he is one of the good ones. We don't want to lose him." Of course, the reason she was an intern at all is that the previous youth minister, Pastor Daniel, was willing to give her everything. There were good reasons for that too, and those reasons are why he did not work at the church anymore.

In every way, Samantha looked like a

sweet very young girl. She was petite and slender and she almost always wore very, very short skirts that showed her panties to her Sunday school teachers or to the youth pastor. That is, she showed her panties when she chose to wear them. She had been held back in school so even though she was 18, she was only a sophomore in high school and still in the youth group. Yet her sweet, slender face, her wispy blond hair, and her tiny breasts gave the impression that she was far younger than she was. She was able to beguile boys and men of all ages with a charming innocence that never revealed that underneath she was a dangerous temptress.

Because of her striking beauty and sexuality, she always stood out to male leaders who all had trouble not gazing at her. Even when her powers to seduce older authority figures was compromised by having a woman in leadership over her, her sensual aura even seduced them. When Pastor Daniel was the youth pastor of the church, he was aware that the sexual magnetism of Samantha was powerful. Even his wife, Jill, noticed it and they joked about it. But what Daniel did not discuss with Jill was that Samantha was getting to him each time she came to the youth activities. And Samantha knew it.

Pastor Daniel's life changed on a Saturday morning when he was in his office doing some paperwork. He was the only one there but the rest of the youth staff was coming at two for a meeting about the weekend's activities. When there was a knock on his open door, he was stunned to see Samantha standing there. For Saturday morning, she looked amazing. She was wearing a tiny flowery dress that showed off her thin white legs. "Can I talk to you Pastor Daniel?" she said softly.

Daniel agreed but he made sure the door stayed open. This was a good precaution but it was not as effective because there was nobody else in the offices around him. "Are you ok Samantha?" He asked. She spoke softly with a little emotion in her voice about a boy she had a crush on that had been rude to her when she flirted with him.

"I think he does not like me because I am ugly," she said with a little tear coming down her cheek.

"That is impossible to believe Samantha," the pastor said. "You are a gorgeous young woman. Any boy would kill to be with you," he said, realizing that came out sounding wrong.

"Do you think I am pretty?" the young girl said softly to the youth leader. The pastor's instincts said to get out of there but his eyes were fixated on those sexy legs that were slightly apart. He saw some of her upper thigh.

"I have never seen a prettier girl than you," the hypnotized pastor said as he stood. He pretended to be looking for something in his books but he was really leaning forward to see those sexy legs part a little more. Samantha was not fooled and she knew the holy man was very turned on by her.

Samantha smiled shyly turning in her chair so the minister got an excellent view of her sexy upper thigh. “Please don’t tell anyone, but I have a crush on you Pastor Dan.” Samantha said turning in the office chair as he walked around toward her. The minister decided it was best to take this talk to the courtyard of the church where it was visible to other people. But when he approached the gorgeous and sexy girl in her chair, something else happened that he was not planning on.

Samantha saw that the good pastor had a huge erection. She did not hesitate after seeing that. She reached over and began to massage his cock through his pants. The pastor had a bundle of mixed feelings. This was so wrong and he wanted to stop it but he had never felt so turned on.

“Samantha, this has to stop,” he whispered even as he pushed his pelvis forward toward her and moved it in rhythm to how she was masturbating him through his pants.

Seductively Samantha stood up and pressed against him even as she unzipped his pants. “I want you to take my virginity,” she said in a low whisper. Of course, her virginity had been taken long ago but the lie was part of her seduction. “I’m 18 and I want you Pastor Dan,” she said pulling him toward her as she rolled back on his desk pushing his papers and desk supplies off onto the floor.

The good man never had a chance. Samantha skillfully freed his very hard cock from his pants as she hiked up her skirt and spread her legs. When the pastor saw her sexy pussy engorged and wet, he lost the ability to resist her. He tried to push her away but the sexy high school girl pulled him onto her skillfully so that hard cock was pointed like a missile to her open pussy hole. Dan fell forward because he lost his balance but Samantha reached in, held his shaft, and guided it to her hole.

It found its mark easily and without resistance, that long hard shaft entered Samantha's very wet vagina and slid in deeper and deeper.

"Oh god no."

He felt that wet pussy constrict around him pulling him deeper inside her. She was the first woman he had been inside who wasn't his wife. He got his hands down on the desk to push up and then he made eye contact with the goddess-like girl he was inside.

"Am I sexy Pastor Dan?"

"Oh god yes," he said as his hormones took over. She pulled him down onto her kissing his mouth and felt his hips kick in and began to fuck the student on his own desk. Dan felt that tight pussy stretch as he pounded his cock in and out of it. He unzipped Samantha's dress and pulled it down, revealing her firm but small breasts. His want of her body was out of control and the youth pastor sucked those cute tits and fucked into her harder and harder.

"Oh god, pastorrrrr..."

Samantha cried, arching up to suck in

Mrs. Pastor Glen

The reception for the new pastor and his lovely wife was joyful. Glen Boyd was excited about working with such a well-established youth group. He had his wife, Susan, join him for the interview and he jokingly referred to her as Mrs. Pastor Glen. She spoke of her love of the youth and that she often was able to develop strong relationships and friendships with the young women because she was a safe shoulder to cry on which is important to teenage girls. And when the subject of why the previous pastor was dismissed, Pastor Glen said, "That will never be a problem for me." And he glanced over at Susan. The men on the committee smiled because with a gorgeous black-haired beauty like Susan at home, why would any man need another?

Katy spotted the pastor's wife as soon as she jumped out of her parent's car. "Susan," she called out, and Mrs. Boyd smiled happily to see her and they entered the church together as Katy's parents went about their duties. Susan was a big role model for Katy. She admired the pastor's wife because she was such a good friend and always there to pray with any of the girls in the youth group. But she also admired that Susan was such a gorgeous woman. She was petite but sexy without losing her innocent look about her. Her breasts were perky but small and her hips and butt rounded out her dress perfectly. Too often, Katy had found herself masturbating while imagining the pastor and his hot wife fucking in their home.

"Susan, can we talk about something that is bothering me?" Katy said as they walked toward the youth rooms to set up for the night's meetings. There was some time so Susan opened one of the prayer rooms, which were often used for counseling. They were good because there was a comfortable couch in there for them to pray together and when Susan flipped the "In Use" sign, the door locked so the counseling session would be private.

"Ok, tell me what's going on with you." Susan said warmly sitting on the couch near Katy so the talk would be intimate.

"It is something that happened at school. There is this girl. Her name is Tammy and she and I have been friends from a couple of my classes. Well last Tuesday, we were hanging out in the art room after the class was over. I was finishing my craft and cleaning up and it was just her and me in there. She is real pretty and all and the boys are crazy about her. But out of the blue, she tells me she has a crush on me," Katy said.

"Ok Katy, well that isn't so bad."

"Wait, there's more, then all of a sudden, Tammy kissed me. It wasn't just a friendship kiss," Katy stammered and then she looked down blushing from the admission. Katy tried to describe the kiss with Susan's gentle encouragement but her words were all mixed up. It was clear to Susan that her favorite intern was confused by the feelings of that kiss. While Susan was in every way straight, this was a common issue with young girls so she knew to show compassion.

"I will tell you what," Susan said softly, holding Katy's soft fingers in her hands. "Don't try to tell me about the kiss. You are safe with me here Katy and this is between us so it is ok that I do not tell your parents. Instead, let's try something else. Instead of describing the kiss to me, why don't you show me?" Susan finished.

"Are you sure?" Katy said gazing into Susan's eyes. It was an unusual approach and even Susan was surprised when she said it. She wondered if it was because she always thought that Katy was one of the most beautiful girls in the youth group. She wore her sandy brown hair long and often braided which accented her pear-shaped face and her gorgeous green eyes perfectly.

Susan nodding with a reassuring smile so Katy knew it was not a "kiss kiss." It was just a way of explaining what happened.

Katy trusted her youth mentor so she slowly leaned forward toward the perfectly shaped lips of her youth pastor's wife. Susan was nervous and she felt her heart going in her chest as she leaned in. When their lips met, it felt like fireworks going off. The kiss was soft and tender. Katy started to pull away until Susan gently touched her face and then the kiss continued becoming more caring and wet by the moment.

For Susan, her husband had been the only person to ever kiss her like this. Katy had her eyes closed as her lips parted and her tongue slipped out. Susan responded by instinct and opened her lips feeling Katy's wet tongue slide over her teeth and begin to explore inside her mouth. The woman and the youth girl kissed like they kissed a boy but they felt a new charge of excitement because the lips they were kissing were a beautiful female she cared about.

Susan and Katy were breathing fast and they could feel each other's hearts going crazy in the quiet room. Suddenly the kiss stopped and Katy gasped "Oh god, oh god" ss she tried catch her breath. Katy clung to Susan's body hugging her close and gasping. Just then, Susan whispered, "Katy, are you excited?" She began to kiss her on the ear and neck.

"Oh god, yes," the young woman whispered back, running her hands up and down the housewife's back.

"We should stop," Susan gasped but it was just words because as soon as she gazed into Katy's gorgeous eyes, they kissed again deeper and harder opening their lips wide to let their tongues plunge deep into their wet mouths. Both girls were making soft squeaking sounds when Katy found the zipper to Susan's dress and pulled it down. Susan held the sexy girl in her arms rolling back onto the couch as Katy pulled the dress around revealing Susan's shapely shoulders and the white straps of her bra.

"I am so turned on. Oh my god," Susan gasped as the lustful woman in her took over and pushed the good Christian leader aside. Susan lay back on the couch pulling her dress down from her shoulders so her bra was revealed. It was Katy that felt her own new sexual lust for a woman go wild as she pulled the straps aside and eased the cups off of Susan's perfectly shaped tits. That was when Katy got up on her knees on top of Susan and leaned down and began to suck her tits.

Susan gasped and moaned feeling her nipples inside a sweet girl's mouth being sucked in a way that excited her more than even when her husband did that. Reaching down she pulled Katy's skirt up over her panties and ran her hands up and down her sexy round thighs. Then without even knowing what to do next, Katy's instinct kicked in and she pushed her panties down over her shapely ass cheeks letting Susan get to that gorgeous butt.

Katy sat up on her knees looking down at

Susan and her want of that sexy body was overpowering. “Do you want me?” she asked, and then she just smiled when all that Susan could do to answer was to nod and then lean forward lifting Katy’s sweet church dress up over her thighs and up so the girl could take it off over her head. As she did that Susan moaned and rubbed the girl’s sexy flesh kissing her stomach and undoing her bra. Katy cried out softly as she felt her church mentor suck her tits and watched as she wiggled out of her panties.

“Pastor Glen loves to lick my pussy while we 69 and I suck his hot cock,” Susan whispered as she pulled Katy’s panties off. Katy leaned over and kissed Susan legs putting her round thighs over Susan face and lowering his wet pussy to her mouth. Outside the room, the sounds of the youth group were going on and the girls heard Susan’s husband and Katy’s parents talking and laughing. But that did not keep Katy from plunging her mouth into Susan’s cunt and licking her slit and clitoris like a real lesbian.

Susan knew what felt good when her sexy husband went down on her so she found Katy’s stiff clit and licked and bit it. She pulled open that sweet young cunt and found her tight pussy hole and licked all around the rim. Katy arched up and moaned out “Oh my god!” when she did that and then again when Susan slid her finger up inside that virgin pussy opening.

That drove Katy wild diving into Susan’s cunt licking and pushing her finger in and out of her oozing vagina as well. Suddenly Katy was overwhelmed and pushed up on her arms and gasped like she could not catch her breath. "Quietly Katy!" Susan gasped also feeling her own orgasm coming. Both girls had their lips on each other's clits when those orgasms hit causing Susan and Katy to bunk into each other mouths wildly and to ooze the juices of each other's cum onto their tongues for their lover to taste and swallow.

Pastor Glen

"Mrs. Henderson, have you seen Susan?" Pastor Glen said to his faithful volunteer.

"You can call me Amanda, Pastor Boyd," she answered. "Is there something I can help you with?"

"Only if you call me Glen, Amanda," the handsome pastor answered, smiling his drop-dead gorgeous smile. "Well Susan usually listens to my talk on Wednesdays and helps me iron it out but she is probably busy with one of the girls right now," he said standing outside the prayer room door where Susan and Katy were exploring each other's pussies.

"I would love to hear your talk Glen." Amanda said with enthusiasm. "I love your sermons. They are always so inspirational."

"That would be so great Amanda. That way I can let Susan finish with whatever girl she is with," the pastor said. "We can use my office."

When Amanda entered that office, she was so excited. She felt privileged to do something for Pastor Glen that his wife had been doing for him. Once they were in the office, the pastor closed the door so he could concentrate. Amanda sat on a comfortable couch but she sat up prim and proper and kept the church skirt she wore in place and her legs together as a lady does in this situation. Still her skirt only covered to just above the knee and the pastor could still tell that the church mom had sexy legs. That cute church outfit was tasteful but it was impossible to hide Amanda's ample breasts. But the pastor was skilled at noticing such things without anyone else knowing it.

Pastor Glen used a small practice podium and began his talk. He could tell that Amanda was paying close attention and she even smiled and gave little claps at times. As an audience, Amanda was far more into his presentation than Susan ever was. But it was all new and exciting to Amanda who was following the thoughts but also thinking how amazingly handsome and sexy the good pastor was. Without meaning to, Amanda let her hips rock back and forth and she felt a little moisture in her panties from the excitement of being alone with him.

The pastor focused on his thoughts but he could not miss the swaying of Amanda's hips as she listened. There was a sensuous movement to it so it wasn't frantic like she was in some kind of distress. And while Amanda was the perfect example of a moral Christian woman, wife, and mom, she was not aware as she wiggled in front of that handsome youth pastor that her legs opened from time to time letting him look up her skirt to see her sexy naked thighs and the white panties that barely hid her sexy pussy that was already wet from the experience.

Glen saw that sexy panty-covered cunt and in spite of himself and he became aroused. He suddenly was aware how dangerous it was to be alone with this woman and to notice that he was getting a hard-on. He tried to cover it up but his dress slacks were not made to hold in a very large cock as it got harder and harder.

As he finished, he smiled at Amanda and she blushed. "Well, we should get back to the kids," he said walking toward the door.

"Yes," Amanda said gasping. "I am sure that Katy is out there somewhere." It was then that she noticed the huge bulge in his pants. She tried to ignore it as she stood up to turn toward the door behind her. Just as he reached the couch, Amanda felt a little light-headed and her foot snagged on the strap of her purse and she began to fall.

"Oh Amanda," the pastor gasped and he caught the church mom by the arm to keep her from hurting herself. There was no way to completely stop the fall but he let her fall toward him, which pushed him backward. His back hit the couch as Amanda fell onto his body. Just then, the zipper of his pants broke from the pressure of his hard-on and his pants opened allowing the hard cock to push out the top of his underwear as he fell onto his back on the couch.

Amanda saw that huge hard cock and she gasped loudly. The office was a little out of the main part of the church so nobody heard her little exclamation of surprise. But her own fall was still not controlled and she rolled off of the couch and landed on the floor of the office. Her skirt flipped up to her hips and the brown skin of her thighs was revealed along with the folds of her pussy that were outlined by the very wet fabric of her panties.

The good man in Pastor Glen thought about her safety first and he rolled toward her. “Amanda, are you ok?” he said. But when he saw her sexy thighs wide open and the bulge of her cunt, the sinner inside him rolled over on top of her. When their bodies stopped, he was crouched over her with one leg on each side of her round hips and his long hard cock angling down to the fabric of her soaked panties. Amanda and the pastor gazed into each other’s eyes both lustfully and fearfully because they were both in such an exposed situation. And neither knew what to say.

“Amanda,” the pastor gasped but he had no words. Just then, he felt her fingers on his hard cock. Amanda responded to that erection the way she would for her husband when he was hard like that.

“Let me be the servant girl of the Lord,” she said with no idea where that came from. Then as she stroked his hard cock up and down, the faithful married pastor kissed her hard and squeezed her tits through her church dress. Amanda moaned with passion knowing she was committing adultery. The guilt of that could not stop her other hand from pushing down her panties to allow her pussy to be available to the holy man.

Neither Amanda nor the pastor had ever fucked anyone but their spouses but their lust was overpowering. Glen saw Amanda working down her panties so he knelt between her open thighs, pulled them down to her knees, and then off. Amanda spread her legs to let the pastor of her children see her very wet pussy. Glen saw Amanda reach between her legs and spread her pussy lips and when he saw that sexy pink cunt hole, he was unable to keep from pushing his pants down more to have enough movement to fuck her.

"Oh Pastor Glen," Amanda moaned as he leaned in and kissed her mouth and moved his hips down to get his erection ready to penetrate her.

"I shouldn't fuck you," he whispered sucking her earlobe and her neck.

"You shouldn't fuck me," she repeated holding his rock hard cock and moving the head to her eager hole. As soon that the big head of the holy man's hard cock found her mommy pussy hole, it drove inside her. The pastor reached down and grasped Amanda's butt cheeks pulling her pelvis up to him. Then he began to fuck in and out of her faster and faster. Her insides were full of such a hot and wet suction that is seemed even her pussy was sucking his cock.

"You shouldn't fuck me," Amanda gasped thrusting up to him. "You shouldn't...you shouldn't...fuck me. Fuck me...fuck me," she said louder and louder. "Oh god fuck me

Pastor Glen!" she said, pushing up to him and thrusting back to his surging cock so they fucked each other in perfect sync.

"I shouldn't cum in you Amanda," he groaned, feeling his balls beginning to push his load up the shaft.

"Don't come in me pastor. Don't... Don't... Don't," she said kissing him and holding to his firm body. "Cum in me... Cum in me... CUM IN ME NOW PASTOR GLEN!" she moaned so loudly that down in the youth center they heard something. Just then, she came with an explosion of writhing and wetness in her cunt and he doubled over and shot his load deep in her pussy, filling it full of his cum.

13 THE BOY BAND

Faye was with the Fresh Boys from the beginning. John, Duke, Aaron, Quinn and Matthew became one of the biggest boy bands in the world and the money flowed in like a waterfall. Faye was so excited for her boyfriend, John, when the band began to achieve success. It made her mad that people said they were only successful for their good looks. She knew that every one of the boys in that boy band were talented and worked hard to be successful.

She knew that Isaac did an amazing job as their manager getting them the inside track in the music business so they could get the national attention they needed. She also knew that every boy in that band was breathtakingly sexy and cute too. That didn't hurt.

They were all amazingly talented and cute

and their image with the public as squeaky-clean. They all wore purity rings to show they promised God they would wait until marriage before having sex. That helped the band because church girls and their mommies saw them as safe and the kind of role models for boys to treat girls with respect and to wait until marriage for sex. But at the shows, the sexual energy was like an explosion.

Faye watched from behind the curtains and she could see young girls go into literal orgasms watching her boyfriend and the rest of the band perform. More than one mom responded that way too. It was like those purity rings made the boys even more exciting to their young fans. Sadly, Faye had seen girls going into dressing rooms of the different boys and come out with that freshly fucked look. Faye stayed close to John to keep girls and women who were nothing more than groupies away from him. But she couldn't be everywhere and it worried her.

The young girls threw themselves at John, the lead singer and her boyfriend. Many times as Faye fought to keep John pure so he could honor that ring that they both wore, Faye wondered if she was losing. It wasn't that she wasn't attractive. Her tall slender figure drew looks from John and the other band members also. John often said he could break her in half she was so slim but her ample breasts resting on that thin frame only made her sexier.

She knew she excited John when they

kissed because she felt his hard on pressing through his pants. Refusing to fuck him because of her commitment to her mom and dad to stay pure until marriage was becoming harder to do. In addition to the pressures he was under, she wanted him inside her in the worst way.

Isaac Helps Out

The New Jersey show sold out the arena that seated 17,000 so fast that they booked another show the next night. It sold out too. To the world outside, The Fresh Boys were the next big thing but to them, they were a handful of young men and women trying to make this all work. Even their manager Isaac felt overwhelmed by it sometimes and he was 33. This was not his first huge arena show to put a band in and it would not be his last.

Backstage at a huge arena show is hectic. It would be easy to get run over with the roadies flying everywhere. So Isaac always stayed in the executive box behind the stage where he could keep an eye on the band members themselves. He was able to tell if they were doing their routines right or if there were any problems. Also, he could fix up the box in the luxury that he liked including a fully stocked kitchen and bar and a nice couch to catch a nap on during set up. It was all his and the huge money the band generated justified the luxury for their manager.

When those lights exploded and the band hit the stage, even an old pro like Isaac got goose bumps. The boys took the stage with the high-energy show that they had worked so hard to work out. Besides watching the band, it was hard not to notice the young girls going crazy for the boys. When the show was about two songs from the intermission, his cell phone rang. It was Faye.

She was not at the show. The commotion of the show set up was too much for her. So she stayed at the hotel. But she wanted to come down and see John during intermission. She asked Isaac if they could use the executive box for some privacy. Isaac thought the world of Faye and admired how hard they worked to keep themselves pure in the middle of the wild world of popular music. Even as Isaac talked to Faye on the phone, he saw a gorgeous woman who looked like she was around 19 get up on the shoulders of a big muscular guy and lift her top. Her perfect tits flashed for the entire band to see. John stared at that offering that was clearly just for him. Isaac knew that few guys could resist that. He agreed to let the two lovers use his private skybox.

About three songs from the intermission break, as Isaac watched through the powerful scopes in the box, Faye walked in. she looked amazing in her cute short leather skirt and a fluffy white top that showed off her shapely boobs nicely. Before Isaac could stop it though, Faye looked through a second scope. She saw the band finish playing their set and John signaled to the woman to join him backstage. When the sexy woman reached the boy band star, she hiked up that top and John had an up-close view of those glorious tits. Without a thought, he pressed in squeezing her nipples and sucking her neck.

Just then, John realized that he could be seen. But Isaac and Faye both saw him press a back stage pass and the key to his dressing room into the sexy girl's hand. Faye pushed the scope away from her face and leaned forward on the shelf below the window that looked down on the stage. The boys were coming back out to start the second half of the show.

As Faye leaned on that shelf, Isaac noticed how great her butt looked in that sexy leather skirt. He scolded himself for getting an erection being alone with her and attempted to be just a friend. He gently put his hands on the sounders of the sobbing girl and massaged them.

"How could he do that Isaac? Am I not sexy enough?" she said through her sobs.

"Faye you are incredibly sexy," Isaac said leaning in to whisper it in her ear. "I see all the guys in the band and the roadies staring at your sexy body." As soon as he said that, Isaac sensed that Faye was breathing harder. She leaned back against him and the feel of her sexy body pressing aroused him.

"I don't think John thinks I am sexy." She said rubbing her butt against his pants. His erection pressed against his pants and she felt it as she wiggled. Faye felt Isaacs hands slide around her middle and hug her close.

"If he doesn't see that you are sexy, he is insane." Isaac said softly as he began to kiss her neck.

"I feel sexy," the young girl cooed, not even thinking about what was going on and just enjoying the tender seduction of a man she liked and trusted. His lips on her neck kissed up to her ear and then sucked the lobe, which sent electric surges of desire through her body. Faye was wigging against the band manager feeling wet and very aroused.

"I am so turned on for you Faye," Isaac said, slipping his hands under her top to feel her tummy.

"I am nervous," she whispered as she looked back at him. Her angelic face melted him and he kissed those sweet lips softly. At the same time, he let his hands side up to cup her breasts under the top. Faye didn't have a bra on so he was able to stroke the soft and warm flesh of her tips and fondle her sexy nipples. "Do I make you hard?" she said gasping.

"Yes baby, you do," he answered and he stood back so she could turn around. As she looked down, Isaac unzipped his pants and pulled out his rock hard, nine-inch penis. The gasp that Faye made filled the room. He took her hand and put it on the shaft and Faye slowly explored the hard cock up and down the shaft and stroked the tip with her delicate fingertips.

He leaned in, kissed her deeply holding the back of her head, and thrust his tongue into her mouth lustfully. The little squeals and squeaks of delight and joy turned Isaac on so he lifted her up onto the counter with the glass behind her that he used to look down on the performance area.

"I want to fuck you Faye," he moaned as his passion took over.

"Oh God, yes," she answered and her legs opened wide for him by instinct. Shaking with excitement, Isaac pushed Faye's skirt up her naked legs revealing the white flesh of her round thighs. Faye watched his hard cock sway back and forth as she leaned back on her hands to give her body to him. Faye came to the stadium to finally have sex with John so she did not have panties on.

As soon as Isaac saw her bare cunt between those milky thighs, he moaned with lust. He leaned in and kissed her hard as the fingers of his right hand plunged into the pussy massaging her clit and pushing open the sexy folds of her cunt. As soon as a finger found the hot wet hole of her vagina, it slid inside her causing Faye to lean back and moan loudly with passion.

Isaac could hold back no more. He moved his cock to her opening and insert the tip into Faye's waiting insides. Slowly he penetrated her deeper and deeper. Faye pulled up her top to let Isaac see, and then kiss and suck, her eager tits. She felt like she might hyperventilate as his cock sucked its full shaft inside her and he began to fuck her.

Isaac's want of Faye's pussy overpowered him. He fucked into her again and again. He forgot to pull out because his orgasm came with such power. It hit him like a hurricane and he exploded inside her filling her with cum.

The Best Thing to Do

Emily did not see herself as a groupie. She knew that the Fresh Boys were a wholesome band. So when she got on her friends shoulders and flashed the band her tits, it even surprised her. She had John's picture up all over her bedroom wall at home. She was 19 years old and stunningly sexy but the only thought that drove her to lie in bed and masturbate was looking at the beautiful face of John from the Fresh Boys.

When Emily returned from making out with John during the break in the show, she showed the key to his dressing room to all of her friends. The squeals of "OH MY GOD" almost broke eardrums in that hall. All through the rest of the show, Emily stared at John's pants thinking about if this could mean he would actually fuck her. It was so hard to concentrate on the show so when it seemed like it was close to time; Emily slipped out and made her way backstage.

The roadies and security recognized she was the one that John was kissing and feeling up earlier and they were happy to guide her to his dressing room. She let herself in with the key John gave her and tried not to go crazy with excitement at what in store for her. She didn't have to wait long. John wrapped up the show and told the guys he felt tired so he could get to the dressing room fast.

When he opened that door and saw Emily, John became instantly turned on. At first both John and Emily were shy even though both of them know what to do. They exchanged greetings and Emily shared how much she adored John and his music. It was when John said, “Oh my God, Emily you are so pretty and sexy” that the sexual energy exploded. They kissed and lowered themselves to a couch that was in there for John to take naps. As John pushed his tongue into her mouth, he felt Emily unzip his pants and reach in.

After Isaac fucked her, Faye was shaking like a leaf. It was all so overwhelming. Isaac was a real gentleman and she knew nobody would know what happened that day. But she could not get out of her mind that now that the concert was over, John and that slut were probably fucking in his dressing room. She decided she had to go there. As she walked, she thought about if she should have a scene. But she was still turned on from having Isaacs's big cock in her. Finally, she decided that maybe the best thing she could do was to not be angry with the boy she loved.

When she got to the dressing room, the door was locked. But security knew Faye was with John so they let her in. There was a short dark hallway with closets and a table before she entered the big dressing room area. But as soon as Faye entered, she heard the moans of passion. Before John or Emily knew she was there, Faye gasped as what she saw. John was lying on the couch and the gorgeous blond girl had pulled his pants down so his big hard cock was out. The slut was leaning over it and moving her mouth up and down on it as John moaned.

Faye stayed quiet as Emily sat up and moved to straddle that big erection of the pop star. She pulled up her skirt and her naked butt came into view. Emily had removed her panties while she waited for John earlier. Then she swung those sexy white thighs over his hips and lowered her pussy to his waiting cock. It sank into her wet pussy in one thrust and quickly John began to fuck up into the stunning 19-year-old fan.

Faye could see it all. She could easily see Emily's pussy hole stretched around John's thick cock as it thrust up into her over and over again. In spite of herself, Faye pulled up her skirt, reached into her panties, and began to stroke her clit watching John hammer his cock in and out of the sexy girl. Just then, John saw Faye in the doorway with her hands in her panties. They made eye contact but John did not stop fucking the teenage fan. Instead, he gestured for Faye to come closer.

Emily was so on fire as she fucked down onto her pop hero that Faye was close before she noticed her there. "It's ok, that's my girlfriend," John said as he leaned up and sucked Emily's left nipple lustfully. "Don't stop."

Faye was hypnotized by the sexy vision of the cute girls cunt stretched around her sweetheart's hard cock. Without thinking, Faye reached in and touched Emily's pussy stroking up and down the pink flesh of the inner slit. When her finger began to caress John's slick cock as it came out of Emily, he groaned, "I'm going to cum."

Faye looked at John's balls and she didn't want him to cum inside of the beautiful girl on top of him. She went to her knees beside the couch, pushed Emily's butt up as John pulled back to thrust again. When she did that, John's slick and hard cock slipped out of the insides of the young fan. Faye grasped that hard cock and the wetness oozed onto her hand. Then she did what she had heard about when a man is about to cum. She put his cock in her mouth.

Faye tasted that wetness when she had a quarter of John's cock in her mouth and something about it being the wetness from inside of Emily excited her tremendously. She began to run her tongue up and down John's hard cock sucking it like a lollipop. Suddenly a huge shot of cum filled her mouth. The cum was hot and sticky and slid into Faye's throat before she knew it. So she swallowed and then as each squirt of sperm came out of her man, she swallowed it right down.

Emily got off of John, turned, and gasped at how gorgeous Faye was. Neither girl had ever had a bisexual experience but seeing the cum oozing out of Faye's lips put Emily into a frenzy. She pulled Faye to her and kissed her lifting Faye's top to strip her while pulling her to the couch.

John slipped off of the couch to the bathroom for a moment. When he returned, Emily was sucking Faye's tits and Faye was pushing her fingers into Emily's cunt from behind to finger fuck her. Any thoughts of an after show party for John disappeared instantly because he had a huge party going on right here in his dressing room.

The Contest Winner

The image of the Fresh Boys was wholesome and pure because that sold a lot of records to middle school moms and their daughters. Of all of the members of the band, Duke tried to maintain the good boy image of the band.

The other guys often enjoyed the bodies of their fans but Duke tried to keep his vows of celibacy. The band hosted about 15 contest winners and their guardians to front seat tickets to the show, back stage passes and a visit to the bands luxury suite. Duke took the lead with that project because it was something he enjoyed doing. Also, the marketing research guys had learned that Duke was the favorite with the moms of the young fans because he was so clean cut.

When Courtney won the prize of the backstage pass package at the Cleveland show, her mom Alice was almost as excited as the teenager. The rules were that each girl who came backstage would be accompanied by a parent or adult guardian so Alice jumped at the chance to enjoy the prize also. She kept a cool head around Courtney but Alice was as big a fan of the Fresh Boys music as her daughter was.

The concert was amazing and the seats that Courtney and her mom had were VIP all the way. They enjoyed a limo ride to the concert with special food and even a glass of wine or two for the moms in the limo. Alice enjoyed that wine very much. In every way Duke made the moms and the young fans feel like they were part of the Fresh Boys world with a princess treatment that would not stop.

After the show, the contest winners and their moms got to come back stage and then they were invited to an after concert party at a swanky suite in the hotel where the boys were staying. Of course, it was not a rock and roll party in the traditional sense. It would be a chance for the girls to ask questions of the band, get pictures and maybe a kiss on the cheek from their favorite Fresh Boy.

The suite was amazing and the image that was given to the guests was that all of the Fresh Boys stayed there. It was strictly for entertaining with fully stocked bar for the moms and all kinds of food and healthy drinks for the girls. Duke was a wizard at organizing this. After everyone had a tour, plenty of refreshments and took in the sights from the top floor of the high-rise hotel, two of the Fresh Boys sat down with the girls, took questions, and sang special request songs from their own catalogue or even things the girls wanted to hear. The moms often sat nearby having more wine and refreshments, taking pictures or videos and enjoying the atmosphere.

Alice got up while the girls were enjoying a song by John and Quinn. The other guys took time off and just hung around signing autographs. Duke hardly ever was "on stage" for these session since he was the coordinator. Alice got herself a fresh glass of wine and began to wander around checking out the suite.

"Are you enjoying the evening Mrs. Gordon?" Duke said entering the kitchen where the two of them were alone.

"It is wonderful. Courtney will remember this forever," Alice answered flushed at being alone with the handsome pop star.

"Well I am glad you both could come," Duke said politely but Alice noticed that his eyes wandered to her chest briefly. Alice was a stunning woman with an amazing bust line that men could not resist. Her husband had a time with guys coming on to her. She was only 32 and she always dressed to show off her round hips and ass.

"The girls have such crushes on you boys," Alice continued. "It is good you are moral boys because you could have any one of your fans." She said feeling herself flushed at speaking so boldly.

"Well we adore our fans in the right way. We would never take advantage of their loyalty inappropriately," Duke answered.

"Yes it would be so easy to win one of

your fans...." Alice continued feeling the wine starting to talk. "Or their mothers," she said with a soft giggle. That comment got a genuine blush from the pop star.

"Well many of the mothers are very beautiful. There is no denying that," he said, gazing at Alice and letting the mild flirtation go on. Alice felt encouraged by that response and slowly crossed the kitchen to him.

"A mother could get very turned on by a handsome pop star like you," she said reaching him and leaning in toward him. Duke had been flirted with before but the privacy of the moment was making him let his guard down. The fact that Alice was so amazingly sexy that he was having trouble hiding his hard-on also impaired his good judgment. Their eyes met as Alice got closer and closer.

"I made a vow," he whispered but it was too late. Alice kissed the sexy boy letting her lips part so he could taste her mouth and feel the tip of her tongue on his lips. Duke felt his heart going crazy. For all his experience with fans, this was new. He could not help himself but to kiss her back. As he did that, he felt her hand find his and she brought the fingers up and put them on her right tit over her blouse.

Instinct kicked in and Duke closed his hand over her breasts squeezing it as his gone explored the sexy mom's mouth. "Oh God, Mrs. Gordon," he gasped. "If we got caught, the band would be ruined."

"Then we better hurry," Alice said

unwilling to stop the avalanche of lust they both were feeling. Duke took her hand and pulled her through a door near the back of the kitchen. It opened into a small bedroom for the help working in the suite. Alice pulled his body to her, reached down, and unzipped his pants.

"But your husband..." he objected as she pushed his pants down just enough to release his gorgeous, rock hard cock. She squeezed it and kissed him hard.

"I think about you when he is fucking me," she moaned and she fell back on the bed lifting her legs high so the pop star could see her sexy thighs and her soaked panties barely covering her cunt. "Fuck me Duke. Hurry," Alice moaned like the slutty mom she had suddenly become. The mom pulled up her skirt and opened her blouse to let him have all he wanted of her glorious tits.

With his hard cock waving in front of him, Duke knelt on the bed and slid his hand up Alice's soft sexy thighs to her panties. He yanked them down and threw them on the floor pushing her legs apart to get to that sexy mommy pussy and fuck it. At the same time, Alice got her blouse open and her bra cups down.

Duke gave into raw lust and dove into that cleavage kissing and biting. When he found her wide red nipple and started to suck it, Alice reached in, found his hard cock, and guided it to her cunt hole. His cock was magnificent and much larger than Courtney's daddy. Feeling her nipple sucked and bit, she arched up and moaned as Duke drove his cock into the mommy filling her vagina completely.

Then Duke pushed up and looked down at the amazing sight of his entire cock inside of Alice. He knew this was so dangerous and wrong the only thing to do was to finish it. He fucked the mom faster and faster. His thrusts became powerful and demanding. Alice felt his muscular and trim body inside her and his strong musician fingers finding her ass cheeks to squeeze them and pull her sex to him to fuck her harder.

"Cum in me. I want your sperm," Alice moaned. Duke kissed her on the mouth deep and long and that caused Alice to moan and orgasm hard constricting her eager pussy hole around that big hard erection. She was fucking up to him when his climax hit and he drove every inch of his penis as far in her as he could and pumped massive streams of cum inside the woman.

As soon as he finished cumming, they had to get busy to cover it up. Duke slipped out a side door and Alice entered the kitchen. Neither could exactly walk right because they had fucked each other so hard. It was by far the best fuck Alice ever had but she didn't know if Duke was impressed by her body.

But about a week later, a telegram was delivered to Courtney that convinced Alice that she would be fucking that sexy boy again. It read. "Dear Courtney. We were so glad you joined us for our special evening with our fans last week. Now I have some great news. You have been selected to be the one special fan to go on tour with the Fresh Boys starting next month in Houston. Call the number below to let me know you can be part of the Fresh Boys family. Love Duke."

Courtney squealed with delight. But it was Alice that was thrilled when she read at the bottom of the telegram that read, "Oh and Courtney, Please don't forget to bring your mom."

14 TEACHER'S CONFERENCE

On her first day teaching at her new school, Amanda saw something shocking. It let her know that this wonderful teaching job at the most exclusive preparatory school in the state could also be a very dirty place.

The realization so stunned Amanda she could do nothing more than stare. Stephanie, her best friend from childhood, was having a very dirty experience. All Amanda could do was watch. Stephanie and Amanda had both been offered their first teaching jobs at the Brookline private school just out of college. It was an exclusive prep school for boys and girls in sixth grade through high school. Amanda would take on her first sixth grade class and Stephanie was hired to coach girls volleyball.

It was so exciting seeing her classroom for

the first time and she thought about Stephanie in the athletic department getting to know her way around. When the day was over, Amanda hurried down to the first floor to see her friend and share their first day impressions. Amanda dashed off the elevator to the offices when she heard moaning and she stopped suddenly before rushing in. Then she felt the blood rush out of her face as she looked into the office of the football coach.

The first image she focused on was of her dear friend Stephanie but it was unlike any image she had seen before. Stephanie was leaning forward on the desk, her butt arched up and her head back. Behind her stood Coach Randolph pulling her body to his. Stephanie was thrusting her butt up to his crotch as though she was in heat and he was humping it.

Amanda had never seen her best friend acting like this. There was a raw animal lust to it all that made Amanda instantly wet. The coach was easily their dad's age. He had silver white hair and his shirt was off. His upper body was amazingly muscular and contoured and he used those muscles to pull Stephanie to him. His strong hands grasped her ample tits through her top and massaged them, which made Stephanie moan with desire.

The coach was on top of her like he was making her his slave. His mouth closed on to her neck, and he kissed and sucked it hard making Stephanie moan all the more. Slowly the half-naked man worked his way down to his knees looking up at the round ass cheeks of the 22-year-old girl. He reached up, grasped each round butt cheek, and squeezed it firmly which made Stephanie's knees buckle a bit. Then without hesitation, he worked her athletic shorts and underwear down her round white legs inch by inch until the crack of her ass and the bulge of her cunt was visible to him and to Amanda watching from a safe distance.

Pulling open her ass cheeks, the older man stared up into the engorged pussy lips of Amanda's best friend. He could not hold back any longer. Standing he pushed down his own sweat pants and his jock. The size of his rock hard penis made Amanda gasp. It jutted out from his hips like a firm pole aimed directly at Stephanie's soft pussy lips.

Coach Randolph leaned in and dominated the young volleyball coach pulling her hips up to him so the spread pussy would open up to him. "Oh God YES!" Amanda heard her friend moan as that big hard cock pressed through the round lips of her open cunt.

"What do you want sexy girl?" the muscular man whispered.

"Fuck me Mr. Randolph," Stephanie said gasping for air as she lifted her ass to him. "Please fuck me now," she moaned like a whore. The football coach was ready to grant her wish. He shifted his hips and then thrust. Amanda saw Stephanie arch back, eyes wide as she felt that large hard-on open her up and fill her wet insides.

Stephanie put her face down in her hands on the desk as the powerful man began to thrust his erect member deep into her pussy hole. He latched on from behind and fucked her with a fury moaning and humping with animal lust. Amanda could hear the sucking sound of Stephanie's hole closing up as he pulled out and then being fully filled with each penetration again and again and again.

With a suddenness that surprised all three, Mr. Randolph began to gasp like he was having a medical problem. Instead, he stood up and held Stephanie and fucked her harder and harder. "I am going to cum!" he moaned and it was too late for anything to stop it. He fell on her burying the full shaft in the young woman filling her with his seed.

The Passage of Time

The first year of teaching was flying by. While the incident with Mr. Randolph was distracting, both Amanda and Stephanie knew that teaching at Brookline was the job of a lifetime. Mr. Randolph left the school under a scandal about a month after he fucked Stephanie in his office. It was a financial scandal but it did help to make that event disappear into the passage of time

Both Stephanie and Amanda took to their jobs like they were born to do them. The campus of Brookline was phenomenal. It was a gorgeous layout of high rises and then acres and acres of open land that was perfect for field trips, athletics or nature walks. But the primary classrooms were all housed in one very well secured high rise where no expense had been spared. Each floor was a separate grade. The top floor was administrative offices and the library.

The next floor down was the 14th floor and it housed the 6th grade classrooms where Amanda worked. Each floor down was a different grade. The lower floors had assembly rooms, the art department, the theatre workshops, several auditoriums and conference rooms and the athletic department on the ground floor where Stephanie worked.

As Amanda set her room up for the teacher's conferences a month out from the end of the first semester, she thought back on how far she had come. She was a success and she loved her kids. But it was the volunteer parents that made it all work. There were several class moms who came to class regularly each week to help with keeping the class organized and to help out if a kid needed to run to the nurse.

Of those class moms, Julia, was one that Amanda struck up an instant friendship with. Julia was the wife of the most prominent local minister who was the head pastor as the Methodist church. Amanda had even begun attending services at the Methodist church because she found such a warm friendship with Julia.

The teacher's conferences went well. It seemed if the dads came, they went particularly well. It did not escape the dads that Amanda was pretty and shapely. She was taller than most girls her age and her slender frame accented her round hips, butt and pert breasts. Her long black hair was striking and it framed her face nicely, showing off her high cheekbones and her long neck.

Amanda deliberately scheduled the teacher's conference with Julia last because she knew it would be so enjoyable to further their friendship. By 8 o'clock that night, they were done but Julia and Amanda had finished the conference part. Julia arranged for her 12 year old, Ashley, to go home with her best friend Beth. Ashley went home with a glowing review from her teacher. The girl was a genuine joy to have in class.

"Ashley just loves you," Julia said smiling a gorgeous smile that lit up the room. She was shorter than Amanda with a cute short haircut so her beautiful blond hair shaped her face and curled in to her neck under her head. She had a nice figure that often drew the attention of the men in the church but she was fanatically faithful to her husband and his ministry in the church.

"She is a prize," Amanda answered sincerely. "As is her mom. I don't know how I would have made it in my first year without you here as the class mom Julia."

That complement touched the tender heart of the preacher's wife and she hugged her daughter's teacher warmly. That hug cemented their already growing friendship. When Julia ended the hug, she noticed a little tear in the eye of that sweet young thing who taught her sweet girl. Julia touched that tear and took it on her finger.

"Your conferences are over. My husband has committee meetings all evening. Would you like to come out to the house for a bit, maybe a glass of wine?" she offered.

"That sounds wonderful!" Amanda said without reservation and she was thrilled for the chance to get to know the minister's wife better. Their house was beautiful and large and as soon as Amanda arrived, young Ashley and her friends came down the stairs in a stampede for hugs. That filed Amanda with pride that she was so well liked. When the girls got done with their greetings, they stampeded off all giggles as fast as they came.

Amanda settled on a big over stuffed couch in the family room as Julia shut the big wooden doors to shut out the sounds of teenage girls having fun together. She asked Amanda what kind of wine she preferred and Amanda asked for Shiraz. "Oh, I love that too." Julia said bringing two large glasses.

They talked through two glasses of wine and before long, they were feeling a bit giggly. Julia was a true pastor's wife showing Amanda real affection and caring. Amanda talked about her desire to be a wife and mom and her longing for that.

"Oh it is a wonderful gift from God Amanda. You will be an amazing wife and mother," Julia said, touching Amanda's hand that rested on her knee just below her skirt. Amanda turned her hand up and their fingers intertwined on her knee.

"Oh Julia, you are such a wonderful friend. I am so lucky to have you," Amanda said and she leaned forward. Julia accepted that hug and it was warm and lasting. Amanda could hear the clock ticking on the wall behind her. As their hug slowly ended, Julia felt the emotions were strong so she gently kissed her friend on the cheek.

As the hug ended, Amanda gazed into the eyes of the beautiful minister's wife. Amanda felt very emotional. Suddenly without thinking, Amanda kissed Julia on the lips. It was a light kiss but it was a kiss. What surprised Amanda is the mom did not get angry or stop the kiss. It was brief but full of feeling.

"I'm sorry," Amanda whispered.

"Don't be," Julia whispered back, and then she kissed her friend's lips again. Amanda could feel both of their hearts beating through their chests. Suddenly both women were overcome with chronic blushing. Amanda put her hands on her face facing forward and Julia just covered her mouth in surprise.

"I have never done anything like that," Amanda said.

"Me either, Amanda. Our church condemns all same sex activity and it never crossed my mind. Even as we were kissing my mind and spirit was going wild inside me," Julia said.

"Are you angry with me?" Amanda asked with her voice quivering.

"It wasn't your fault or my fault. It just happened. But no, sweetie. I have never felt closer to someone other than my husband," Julia answered.

"Will you hold me?" Amanda said with a voice that was small like a little girl's. Julia opened her arms to her friend and Amanda entered the comfort of her arms. Slowly Julia lay back on the big pillows of the couch and held Amanda petting her hair and humming softly. Amanda began to relax knowing the feelings were strong but not overwhelming. That is when she looked up from Julia's shoulder to her eyes.

Their eyes met. Suddenly the motherly Julia felt new feelings. Her lips were drawn to Amanda's like it was an unstoppable force. The kiss was instantly passionate. For Julia the only kiss of its kind was the ones she shared with her husband but he had long stopped kissing her like that. The passion the moment excited her as a woman as it did when she and her husband dated.

Amanda gave in to the kiss. The soft lips of her dear friend became moist as their lips parted. Looking back, neither remembers who first engaged tongue. Amanda felt the minister's wife explore her mouth with her tongue and Amanda thrust her tongue inside Julia's mouth and pulled it back not sure if this was acceptable or beyond acceptable.

The passion seemed to have a mind of its own. Both women were finding their way in the dark. As Julia arched her head back gasping, "Oh God, help me!" Amanda kissed and sucked her neck. "Amanda we have to stop," Julia begged but as she begged her, she rolled Amanda onto the couch and unzipped the front of her dress.

Amanda pulled her dress open and saw Julia look up hearing the girls giggling upstairs. “This is so wrong,” she said in a whisper and at that Amanda sat up with her dress open and her bra showing.

“I know,” she said putting her hand on Julia’s bare leg just below the end of her skirt. “I am so turned on,” Amanda said in her next sentence and when she leaned forward, Julia kissed her deeply. The passionate woman in each of them was far more in control than the good girls who objected. Julia did not have hose on so when Amanda’s hand slid up her skirt, all she felt was sexy warm thigh. By instinct, Julia parted her legs as she felt the schoolteacher feel her way up her skirt. Julia rolled back, looked up at the ceiling, and moaned opening her legs wide and pulling up her skirt. Her mind was screaming, “You are giving yourself to a woman, stop now.”

But she didn’t stop. Amanda’s fingers reached her panties and rubbed up and down that fabric that was just over her pussy. Her panties were soaking wet. “You are so sexy Julia,” Amanda said, shocked as the words came out and at that her fingers slid inside the married woman’s panties and she began to explore the folds of her cunt.

“Take my panties off,” Julia gasped, arching her hips up and allowing her pretty dress to ride up showing almost all of her sexy white legs. Before the skirt was up all the way, Amanda worked Julia’s panties over her legs and ripped them from her body. "Do you want me?" Julia gasped to her new lover.

"So much. This is so new to me," Amanda said pulling her own dress from her shoulders so it could fall off showing her bra.

"Show them to me." Julia said sinfully and Amanda obeyed pulling her bra from her shoulders and unsnapping it so it fell away. Her pretty small breasts were viewable to Julia with her dark nipples standing out with arousal. Julia opened her arms to her even as Amanda's fingers found her wet pussy. The women kissed moaning and Amanda unzipped Julia's dress. Between them, Julia's fingers were playing with Amanda's tits.

Amanda sat up a bit to look down at the trimmed pubic hair of the married woman and the open slit she was stroking. Julia's clit stood out and Amanda stroked it. Just then, she felt Julia lean forward and begin to kiss her breasts. Amanda looked down and gasped as her right nipple disappeared into Julia's mouth. The minister's wife sucked her friend deeply rubbing her tongue on the end.

Just then, Amanda found the wet opening to Julia's pussy and her finger slid inside her easily. When Julia felt penetrated, she arched up to her lover pushing her hips up to accept Amanda's fingers.

"Oh yes, fuck me darling," the religious woman moaned out of her mind with passion. Julia's white legs were wide open and Amanda watched her fingers disappear inside thrusting in and out of her.

At the same time Julia's hand found Amanda's thigh as she knelt on the couch over Julia and instantly it shot up her leg to her panties and slid inside feeling and poking the younger girls pussy eagerly. Amanda looked down seeing the pastor's wife's hand in her panties and opened her legs wide. In just second, Julia found Amanda's vagina and pushed her finger into it.

Amanda knelt over Julia with her fingers inside her wet pussy and Julia bucked with wild passion as she finger fucked Amanda. Their passion picked up both of them thrusting their pelvises out in rhythm with each thrust. Suddenly Julia arched up and moaned so loudly the kids heard it upstairs and thought, "Is an animal outside?" She came hard bending over and oozing her orgasm all over her lover's hand.

That was all Amanda could stand and she came also. She reached down and pushed her fingers through her panties and against Julia's knuckles to help Julia probe deep in her cunt and then she fell forward cumming in spams. Amanda fell onto the mother of her student kissing her deeply as both left their fingers inside each other.

The Power Outage

Life changed on the inside dramatically for Julia but she was skilled at keeping her new passion for Amanda hidden from her husband, her daughter, and from the church.

Julia was forever changed in her sexual desires in that hour with Amanda in her own home. Julia lived for those moments when she could be at the school in the classroom just to be close to Amanda. Both women knew they had to avoid another incident that could ruin both of them.

After hours at school, Amanda often found herself on the phone with Julia and the tears flowed on both ends. Julia confessed to Amanda that she felt she had fallen in love with the young teacher. It was common for those talks to become so intense that Amanda would have to pull up her skirt at her desk and masturbate thinking of Julia as Julia did the same at her home.

"I love you so much, Amanda." This Thursday night, like many, Amanda intentionally worked late to talk to Julia on the phone.

"I love you too, Julia. I think about you all the time," Amanda whispered back, as her fingers slipped inside her panties and she began to stroke her clit.

"I masturbate to you all the time sweetie," that mature voice on the other end said and Amanda could tell that Julia was masturbating about her too. "I wish you could come over," Julia said with longing in her voice.

"Maybe I can if I leave now," Amanda said because she was unable to contain her desire for Julia any more.

"Hurry darling. Steve will be home soon.

Come make love to me," Julia said excitedly.

Amanda gathered her stuff in a hurry. Outside she heard a storm gathering so she worried about getting stuck in a rainstorm on the way over to see her lover. Just as she was about to dash out, the phone in her classroom rang. She glanced at the caller ID window and it said Principal Janson. Amanda knew she had to take that call.

"Miss Hanson, I have good news for you," the principal said. "The school board has approved your funds for the science project for the full amount of $250. I am about to go home but if you meet me in the library, you just have to sign a couple things and we can get the materials ordered in time for when your kids are ready to start their projects."

Amanda knew she had to run up to the library and sign those forms and she was excited that the projects were approved. She put all of her stuff at the end of her desk so she could grab them and run to Julia's as soon as she got back.

As soon as Amanda walked into the library, she gasped seeing Mr. Janson. He was a tall lanky man in his 60s and his hair was pure white and combed straight back. Amanda had always had a "thing" for older men. She adored her father and they were very close. Her dad died when she was in her first year of college. That was a horrible year for Amanda trying to cope to life without him.

Amanda's feelings for her dad were always very pure and sweet with no hint of anything inappropriate about them. It wasn't until about a year after the passing of her father that Amanda noticed her tremendous attraction to older men especially with grey hair. The "flings" she had with professors or other older men in college always resulted in much more powerful orgasms.

But that had been a while ago and with all of the excitement in her life since starting work as a teacher, she had almost forgotten that attraction. When she walked into that library and looked at the sophisticated and handsome figure of Mr. Janson, it all came rushing back.

"Come in Miss Hanson, this won't take long and we can be on our way," the principal said, smiling at Amanda. Amanda was suddenly aware that she had worn a short skirt that day and that she was showing a great deal of thigh as she sat down. It only took a few minutes to sign the proper forms to release the funds for the science projects. Amanda was glad because she found herself breathing faster being in his presence and she was eager to get on her way to go see Julia.

As they packed up to leave, there was a sudden crack of thunder from the storm outside. "Oh it is stormy," Mr. Janson said pulling an umbrella from his things. "Let's ride down the elevator together. I can escort you to your car," he said chivalrously, and they stood to go with Amanda leading the way.

Suddenly a huge crack of thunder hit and there was an explosion followed by popping all over the room. The building rocked from the explosion of a generator after it was hit by lighting and the building was suddenly cut off from power. The library went dark except for the dim light of the emergency exit lights.

Amanda heard herself scream with fright as the violence of the lightning strike threw her to the floor of the library. Just as suddenly, Mr. Janson was thrown on top of her and the two educators were floundering around on the floor trying to figure out what happened. Amanda felt Mr. Jansen's arms over her, as he seemed to be shielding her body from any falling objects that may have been shaken loose by the explosion.

For a moment, the two laid there him on top of her breathing heard and listening to try to figure out if more explosions were coming. They heard sirens and that did not help cut down on the fear. In all the falling, Amanda's short skirt had pushed up over her hips so all of her brown thighs were out in the open. As she lay there, Amanda was aware of her skirt.

Almost at the exact same time, Mr. Janson and Amanda realized that his right hand was on her thigh. During the fall, Amanda's skirt had pushed up to her panties and his hand was only a few inches below the roundness of her ass cheek in that flimsy cotton undergarment. His other arm was over her and holding himself up a bit so as not to crush the cute young teacher under his body.

Amanda felt a surge of excitement feeling

that hand on her leg particularly when the principal did not move it. Mr. Janson was feeling excited, too, in spite of the fact that he was a happily married man of 40 years. He had never cheated on his wife who he adored and to be turned on for this sexy young teacher was totally against school policy.

It was quiet and his hand did not move. The principal was also aware that he was holding the soft and sexy thigh of his 6th grade teacher. Both of their breathing was labored. Amanda pushed around so she could turn and look into his face. His lines and that white hair along with that hand on her leg got to her. As their eyes locked, their faces grow closer and closer.

Mr. Jansen was exploding with mixed feelings. This was so wrong and he had been faithful to his wife for decades. But there was no denying the huge reaction that kept growing as he slowly felt up and down Amanda's sexy leg. The magnetism of their lips drawing closer was impossible to resist. All he could do was whisper, "I am so sorry." And then he kissed her.

The kiss was instantly deep and intense. Amanda slid her tongue into his mouth and moaned with passion pushing her butt up to his body. When her butt contacted his crotch, she felt the large bulge of his hard-on through his trousers. The older man was moaning and struggling with his morals and with his body.

As soon as the kiss broke, he repeated, "I'm so sorry Miss Hanson." His apology was ignored as Amanda reached d between them and unzipped his pants reaching in to pull out his rock hard cock. Instinct kicked in as the principle slid his hand up to the perfect ass of the young woman, massaging her butt cheeks he pulled her panties down working them back and forth so they got down to her thighs and gave him access to her sexy cunt.

Amanda kissed her principal again moaning, “I want this so much Mr. Janson. I want to be yours. You can have me. Please take me here. Fuck me sir.” She was out of control with want. Their bodies were in perfect position for intercourse. Amanda moved sideways so her butt was in alignment with his hips and pushed up to him. When the principal first moved his stiff cock to contact the young body of his teacher, it slid into her ass cheeks and briefly contacted her anal opening.

Amanda slid her hand back between her legs and found the dangling hard on and moved it into her pussy slit. She could feel her new lover shaking from the excitement and fear of what was going on so when her fingers closed around his hard cock, he fell on to her and began to thrust without the control he needed. Amanda provided that guidance moving her hips and his hard on together so that in seconds the distinguished principle felt the warmth and wet of Amanda’s oozing cunt begin to draw him inside her.

He thrust and he instantly sank all 7 inches of his hard cock into the young woman. At the same time both Mr. Janson and Amanda arched up and moaned "Oh God" at the sensation of penetration. Then he began to fuck her. At first, he drew out slowly and back in savoring every part of that movement and the feel of the smooth walls of her vagina sucking his hard cock lovingly. But then his intensity increased. He scooped her up to his body and fucked into her again and again and again. His sounds changed to grunts and from her the moans of "Oh Yes, Oh Yes" only made him fuck her more intensely. Amanda was also thrusting back into him matching his motions with her hips to make each movement fill her completely inside.

Amanda's body was on fire as she felt that hard erection fill her deepest places and fuck in and out of her. She unbuttoned her dress in front and pulled down her bra as her older lover held her and instantly his fingers found her naked breasts squeezing them and stroking her hard nipples. It was when Mr. Janson took her left nipple in his fingers and rolled it that she orgasmed for the first time gasping and bucking up to him as her climax shook her hips and cunt causing her to constrict around his thrusting cock.

When the senior administrator of the school felt young Amanda cum under him, it brought out the wild animal in him. He hunched into her, thrusting wildly, fucking her hard and fast. Amanda gasped at the fury and power that he was penetrating her. Almost at the exact same moment, on the dark floor of the school library, the school principal came inside of Amanda, which drove her into her second powerful orgasm.

Amanda spread her legs as wide as she could feeling her lover bury every inch of his hot and stiff cock deep into her to fill her with cum. The explosion coming from his balls fired huge streams of cum inside her. It was the most powerful orgasm he had felt since his honeymoon causing him to produce at least double or more the amount of sperm that he ever put inside his sweet wife.

When he finished he fell forward on to Amanda continuing to cum for what seemed like hours. He kissed her back, neck and face enjoying the gentle constricting of her pussy muscles around his convulsing cock deep in her hole.

The Morning After

The lights came on in the library suddenly at 3 a.m. Amanda woke up feeling sore deep in her pussy from the pounding Mr. Janson had given her. She looked over and saw him asleep on his back next to her. The intensity of their orgasms must have worn them both out and they feel asleep in the dark and quiet comfort of the warm library.

Amanda felt a lot of emotions but totally drained and satisfied from the most amazing orgasms of her life. Mr. Janson was still in his full suit but it was rumbled and messy from having sex in it. His suit pants were barely on his but still over his hips. The fly was open and his long, limp penis was laying on his hip resting from the hard work it did inside of Amanda just hours before.

Amanda looked at that limp cock and the memories of how it felt when it was pounding in and out of her excited her. She reached over, picked it up, and gently fondled it in her hand. She lifted it with one hand and with the other, she explored the older man's testicles that had pumped so much cum into her. Suddenly Amanda was aware that her panties were down by her knees so she pulled them up. But she never stopped staring at that limp cock just inches away from her.

Finally, temptation was too much. She remembered that it was 3 a.m. and they were in the school library, she knew that nobody was in the building so she had perfect privacy. Quietly she leaned over and licked the end of his penis. She knew the wet from inside her cunt had dried on it so it was not smooth. Slipping the tip inside her mouth, she began to enjoy the sensation of sucking his cock and feeling it begin to grow.

Before long, Amanda felt the soft hand of her boss on her hair as she sucked his cock. He was awake and tenderly petting her head, which encouraged her to take more of his now stiff shaft in her mouth and move her mouth up and down on it. When it was completely hard and ready, Amanda was flowing with wetness between her legs and was eager to fuck him again.

"Miss Hanson," she heard him whisper softly. Releasing his hard cock from her mouth, she wiggled up to his handsome face and kissed him all over that face. "Please Miss Hanson," he said with a voice full of emotion. "What I did to you was so wrong," he said expressing his morality.

"The only wrongness about it is if you don't do it again," she said, kissing his lips deeply and pulling him toward her as she rolled onto her back. Mr. Janson was feeling surges of guilt and morality but they were not strong enough to fight the temptation to fuck that sexy 6th grade teacher again. He thrust his tongue into her mouth, kissing her hard as he crawled between her legs and reached into her crotch to pull the fabric of her panties aside.

"Oh yes," he heard the passionate girl moan as his married cock filled up her unmarried cunt all over again. He let himself sink inside her slowly to enjoy every moment of the sensation. The lovemaking was slower and more emotional as the kisses lingered and she opened her top to give him access to her pert tits to kiss and suck. He loved how she held his head and stroked his white hair as he took her nipple into his mouth and tasted it deeply.

Amanda arched up to him kissing and sucking his ear as he sucked down her neck and slowly but forcefully slid his cock in out of her well-lubricated cunt. His hands stroked up and down her thighs and then slide around to grasp her ass cheeks. She squeezed them hard making another soft moan come from the throat of the angel he was fucking. Then he pulled her cunt up to him and began to fuck her faster and faster.

Amanda held his neck and trust back taking all of the cock she could get and pulling him deep in to her. His orgasm took longer but once again, he exploded into her with a powerful eruption of sticky white male seed.

The Missed Appointment

Mr. Janson had the codes and keys to let them out of the building. He and Miss Hanson adjourned to separate bathrooms to clean up and to avoid the temptation to fuck again. And that temptation was strong in both of them. Amanda carefully lined her panties with paper towels to stop the flow of cum that was oozing out of her. He walked to her car and kissed her deeply as the smell of freshly fallen rain filled their nostrils.

"This can never happen again," he said softly at the end of the kiss allowing her reluctantly to leave his embrace.

"No it cannot," she agreed. "But it will," she said with a coy smile.

"Yes," he agreed, knowing what was really in his heart and he walked to his car. Amanda drove carefully home as the night shift workers were getting off work and the early shift laborers were sleepily driving to work.

She stumbled into the apartment she shared with Stephanie and tried to be quiet. It was 6 a.m. and it had been the first time she had been out late in a long time. She got some orange juice and settled back into one of the beanbag chairs in the living room, still glowing with the amazing sex she had gotten from her boss at the school.

"Oh my god," Stephanie said stepping out of her bedroom. "You look so freshly fucked," she giggled.

"That's because I am," Amanda said with that girl-in-love sound in her voice.

"Oh My God for real?" the cute, round, blond girl responded and she rushed to the other beanbag chair to hear all about it. She was not even dressed so she only had on her bra and a tiny pair of panties. Amanda had never shared with Stephanie about her wild sex with the minister's wife and she tried not to let on that she was noticing how cute Stephanie's body looked with so little on.

Amanda began to carefully describe step by step how it came to pass that she got her brains fucked out by the highest administrator in the school.

"Oh God Amanda. That is even hotter than when I…." and then she paused.

"Oh Stephanie, its ok," Amanda said giggling like a little girl. "I know all about that time when Coach Randolph fucked you in his office."

'NO WAY!" Stephanie screeched with delight. "How COULD you know?"

"I watched the whole thing!" Amanda confessed. "And then I had to go and masturbate like crazy because it was so hot to see that," Amanda said sliding her hand up her leg.

"It was SO HOT!" Stephanie said thinking back on that day. "I have never cum so hard girl," she said with a soft moan in her voice.

Amanda watched as Stephanie's hand wandered up her own leg. She was in a dream state remembering bending over that desk and letting that huge cock fill her inside and allow that huge strong coach just take her.

Stephanie ran her fingers over the outside of her panties teasing her pussy that was becoming wet just inside. Then her plump fingers slid inside and she began to feel up and down her slit masturbating to that exciting memory.

Amanda was drawn to that erotic sight of Stephanie feeling herself up. Those panties pulled to the side were showing the puffy lips of her best friend's cunt as Stephanie felt her vagina and then moved her fingers up to her stiff clit that was sticking out just above. Stephanie was also watching her friends sexy legs come into view and then her panties. As Amanda pulled them down, the tissues she used dropped to the ground and her freshly fucked cunt was in full view of her friend.

Both girls felt their breathing deepen and speed up as each watched the other one stroke her pussy slowly enjoying the sensuality of it all. Amanda felt the electricity in her body surge seeing her best friend's eyes glued to her cunt as she stroked her clit. Suddenly Stephanie's eyes grew wide with excitement. She spotted a tiny white trickle of thick fluid making its way out of her roommate's vagina.

"Oh My God Amanda. Is that Principal Janson's cum?" she asked with a gasp.

Just then, Amanda looked down to see the orgasm of her lover coming back out of her after he pumped so much of it inside her only hours before. She had used those tissues to get home without a mess so much of it stayed inside her.

"Oh God, it is!" she said with a gasp of excitement. Without thinking, Amanda slid her fingers down from her swollen clit and slipped one finger inside her pulling out a glom of his sperm. Looking at Stephanie teasingly she put her finger in her mouth and tasted his cum, sucking it clean and swallowing the cum that was on her finger.

"I want to taste it." Stephanie moaned, getting on her hands and knees and crawling toward Amanda's open thighs. Amanda was stunned at how fast Stephanie moved to her pussy. Before Amanda could think about it, Stephanie put her fingers in the open slit of her pussy and rubbed it up and down that pink sensitive skin. Then she slipped her finger inside her friend's hole and pulled out her own serving of cum.

Both girls were on fire with lust when Stephanie put her finger in her mouth and licked it clean tasting the cum that had been deep in Amanda's vagina. Then Stephanie gave in to the excitement and lowered her mouth to Amanda's cunt and began to lick her vagina hole, cleaning up the cum as it streamed out of her. Her tongue wandered from Amanda's clit to her anal rim lapping eagerly and moaning with desire.

Stephanie's fingers were in her own pussy stroking her clit and fingering herself as she ate out Amanda. Amanda stared at her own pussy with that gorgeous face buried in the folds of her snatch licking and sucking. The fire in her loins was taking her over. Before long, Amanda was holding Stephanie's head to push it down into her slit and her hips were pumping up to her with fucking motions that were uncontrollable.

"Oh God Steph!" she moaned. "You are going to make me cum!" Amanda gasped out as best she could but that was all she could say. Her orgasm hit her like a tsunami. She arched up and came hard, creating an ooze of fluid and surged out from inside her and into her sweet friend's mouth.

When the orgasm was done, Amanda fell back in a pile. But her night of wild sex was not done. She looked over at her friend who was lying back on the floor with her back on the beanbag chair and her sexy naked thighs were wide open. Stephanie masturbated herself slowly watching Amanda and smiling seductively. Amanda knew what it meant and even though she had never licked her pussy, the nervousness was taken over by want for the sex of her childhood friend. She got up on her knees and walked on them toward Stephanie.

Just then, she heard a message come in on her phone. Amanda reached over, pulled the phone from her purse, and looked at it. It was a long text from Julia.

"My dearest Amanda," it read. "I cried when you did not come over last night. But I think it was the best thing. I love you so much but I have to think of my husband

and children. Our affair cannot go on. I desire you so much and I am crying now, but before I fall further in love with you we must stop. I am going to take Amber out of the school so you and I are not tempted by each other. Goodbye my love."

Amanda looked up from the text and thought for a second. She had just been dumped. But then she thought of the wild sex she had with Mr. Janson. And then she looked down at the wide-open cunt of her wonderful friend Stephanie just begging for Amanda's lips to lick her to an orgasm. Then she thought, "Wow my lesbian lover just dumped me! Oh Well!" And with that, her face dove into that sexy cunt that was only for her and did not come up for a long, long time.

AUTHOR'S NOTE

Readers: I want to expand a few of the stories to see where the characters can be explored further. If there are any of the stories that you would like to read more about again, I'd love to hear from you!

Visit my blog at
http://www.stefanmckinnis.com

Join my newsletter for free exclusive previews
http://www.stefanmckinnis.com/in

Follow me on Twitter at
http://www.twitter.com/stefanmckinnis

Like my page on Facebook at
http://www.facebook.com/stefanmckinnis

Discover my books at major ebook retailers everywhere.

www.ingramcontent.com/pod-product-compliance
Lightning Source LLC
Chambersburg PA
CBHW020313200626
46814CB00006BA/2232
* 9 7 8 1 6 2 3 2 7 5 7 5 4 *